GRAND OPENING

Come in for a whole new you

Makeovers 20% off

A word from Sharon Harper:

Have you read his list of mistakes on the back cover of this book? Convincing, isn't he? Expects everyone to give him a break because he's a confirmed bachelor. Well, three confirmed bachelor mistakes later, and he still hasn't gotten it right!

Before I met him, I was single and happy. No handsome, sexy man in my life to pine over. No waiting for the phone to ring. No waiting for those three little words.

And now, just when I'm hopelessly in love with the guy, he goes and makes the biggest confirmed bachelor mistake of all time.

He does it in chapter eight. You'll know it when you come to it.

Dear Reader,

As a single woman, I know that trying to meet Mr. Right can be exasperating—and incredibly exciting. Some say love happens when you least expect it. And that's what Yours Truly is all about. A new line of charming, clever love stories in which men and women meet—not only when they least expect to, in *ways* they least expect to.

Take, for example, *Wanted: Perfect Partner* by Debbie Macomber, one of our two terrific launch titles. In this warm, witty novel, a divorced mom meets the man of her dreams through a personal ad that *she* never placed. And in Lori Herter's hip, humorous *Listen Up, Lover,* an alluring written announcement leads California's most confirmed bachelor to walk his very cold feet down the aisle.

You see, Yours Truly characters meet unexpectedly through forms of written communication, such as personal ads, love notes from secret admirers, wedding invitations—even license plates! If you've ever met someone special through written communication, send me a *brief* account (50 words) of your real-life Yours Truly romance. If you include permission for me to edit and print your story, you might see it on a special page in the months to come!

Each month, look for two Yours Truly titles—entertaining, engaging romance novels about meeting, dating... marrying Mr. Right.

Yours truly,

Melissa Senate

Editor

Please address questions and book requests to:
Silhouette Reader Service
U.S.: 3010 Walden Ave., P.O. Box 1325, Buffalo, NY 14269
Canadian: P.O. Box 609, Fort Erie, Ont. L2A 5X3

LORI HERTER

Listen Up, Lover

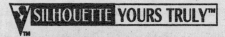

Published by Silhouette Books
America's Publisher of Contemporary Romance

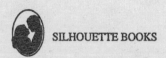

SILHOUETTE BOOKS

ISBN 0-373-52002-6

LISTEN UP, LOVER

Copyright © 1995 by Lori Herter

This edition published by arrangement with Harlequin Books S.A.

Printed in U.S.A.

About the author

LORI HERTER has written three novels for Silhouette Books. What inspired her to write *Listen Up, Lover*? "When I lived in Chicago," Lori says, "I listened to a morning radio show hosted by a popular disc jockey. Every day he'd choose a letter from his mail to read over the air, and since he tended to be a bit chauvinistic, I wrote him a letter of my own, chiding him about that. Wanting to be anonymous, I signed the letter with a funny, made-up name.

"He read my letter to his listeners, bantering back at me—and I was hooked! I wrote several more letters, and each time he responded over the air. I discovered I enjoyed the challenge of writing something entertaining enough for a disc jockey to read over the radio. That discovery led to my becoming a published author years later.

"When I moved to California, I wrote him a farewell letter and signed it with my real name. He read it on the air with a hint of sadness, I thought. I haven't written to a disc jockey since, but that little episode in my life was the inspiration for my career as a writer—and for the story line of *Listen Up, Lover*. Hope you enjoy it!"

Currently, Lori is working on her next novel for Yours Truly, which will be published in February 1996.

1

—◆—

Everyone wants to be at Wanna Be's, Newport Beach's hot new styling salon at Fashion Island shopping center. During Wanna Be's Grand Opening this week, all services will be twenty percent off—everything from perms, foil weaves, tints and cuts, to manicures, complete make-overs, facials, even aromatherapy. Complimentary coffee, tea cakes, and wine will be served, so make an appointment now to pamper yourself under the care of Wanna Be's expert staff. Call Sharon today at 714 555-3131, and begin to be all you want to be at Wanna Be's.

Pushing her long, wavy red hair out of her eyes, Sharon Harper perused the final version of the ad she had just retyped on her ancient, beat-up, Smith Corona portable. She was sitting at her desk in the cubbyhole back room that served as Wanna Be's office. The door was open, and Tiffany Lindstrom, a lithe, shapely, twenty-one-year-old, walked in.

"The painters are quitting for the day," Tiffany said, looking at the sky blue paint smudges on her old Mickey Mouse T-shirt. Her blond hair had been shoved beneath a protective red baseball cap. "They say to tell you they'll do the finishing touches tomorrow."

"Great," Sharon said. "On schedule—I can't believe it! We'll open next week, as planned." She handed Tiffany the sheet of paper she'd taken out of her typewriter. "I wrote this for QWIN radio. Tell me what you think. Be honest."

Tiffany took a few moments to read the paragraph. She nodded with approval as she finished. "It's perfect, Sharon. You've covered all the info, and the last sentence is catchy." She handed the paper back to Sharon. "Go with it."

"Thanks. What a relief to have that done!" Sharon hadn't written anything other than a few letters since graduating high school eight years ago, and preparing her own radio commercial had been an intimidating task. "Rick Slocum suggested I hire an ad agency," she said with a sigh, referring to QWIN's ad salesman. "But they're expensive, and I've sunk all the money I have into the salon. I hope the ad sounds professional enough."

"Sure it does." Tiffany, who wore short shorts, sat on the edge of Sharon's desk and retied her Nike. "Not that it'll matter."

"Won't matter?"

The nubile blonde finished with her shoe and rubbed her nose. "I know you don't listen to rock music anymore, but I wish you'd tune in QWIN's morning show. You should hear Stoney Ross at least once, so you know what he's like."

Sharon lifted her shoulders. "He's just a disc jockey, isn't he?"

"He's the number *one* DJ in Southern California."

"I know," Sharon said. "I checked his Arbitron ratings. My ad will reach the biggest audience. What are you worrying about?"

Tiffany chuckled. "*I'm* not worried. I suggested Stoney's show, didn't I? It's just that he's known for his irreverence."

"I don't care how obnoxious he is," Sharon said. "Just so he does my commercial every day for a week. That's what I'm paying for."

"But sometimes he gets a little fast and loose with the commercials he reads," Tiffany explained. "I don't want you to be surprised. In fact, it might be safer to record it yourself and give them a tape."

"Am I an actress or something?" Sharon said, laughing. "I've barely managed to write the commercial."

Tiffany studied her with a hint of trepidation in her brown eyes. "Okay, but don't get mad if he says something you don't like."

Sharon realized that Tiffany was concerned some off-the-cuff remark from the disc jockey might set her off. She could understand why. Tiffany had seen her fly off the handle at small things several times during the few years they'd worked together at their former employer's hair salon.

"Me, mad?" Sharon said with mock innocence, knowing she'd earned a reputation for her feisty temper dating back to grade school. Lately, however, she'd worked hard to develop more perspective and a sense of humor about herself and about life. She'd hoped her friends had noticed.

"You *have* been so calm lately," Tiffany admitted in an admiring tone. "I haven't seen you blow up at anyone for almost a year. Your yoga and meditation have really done wonders. I wish I had your discipline."

"That's the key." Sharon pointed upward with her forefinger briefly, then put down her hand, realizing she must look like a professor. But she went on to affirm her new approach to life, having such confidence in her daily program that she felt almost evangelistic about it. "At first it seemed like a real pain to practice relaxation techniques every day. But now if something starts to rile me, I do some alternate nostril breathing, turn on some soothing music and in no time I'm as mellow as an old pooch by the fire. I actually feel like a mature adult now instead of an overage adolescent," Sharon said with some pride. "I'm focused. I have priorities and a goal. I feel really together for the first time."

"I'm sure you'll make Wanna Be's a huge success," Tiffany said, her mascaraed eyes widening with ingenuous certainty. She was five years younger than Sharon. "I'm proud of you. You're my role model."

Sharon suddenly felt that maybe she shouldn't brag so much. "Better see if I fall flat on my face with this venture before you make me a role model," Sharon advised with a hint of gallows humor. She might have confidence, but she knew she didn't have much real experience at being a businesswoman. Running her own shop might be more of a challenge than she was ready for, she secretly worried. But it was her dream and she would endeavor to learn all she needed to make her salon a success.

She took the paper and folded it. "I'll give this to Rick Slocum tomorrow."

"I still wish you'd listen to Stoney Ross just once."

Sharon shook her head. "I'm too anxious about our opening to even think of listening to a rock station." She had switched to a New Age station some time ago, because she'd found that rock music made her edgy and contributed to her former, keyed-up personality. "I need to keep mellow."

Tiffany seemed to agree and nodded. "Well, I've got to get ready for Tom. He's coming to pick me up any minute." She took off her hat and her luxuriant hair tumbled down. "Do I look good enough for a pizza parlor?"

"You always look *too* good," Sharon replied with amusement.

Nervous energy kept Sharon reed-thin while Tiffany had the sensual body of a centerfold. Her shining blond hair looked so alluring, she was a walking advertisement for

Wanna Be's. Sharon had to work at looking like a knock-out. Tiffany had been born one.

"Do you have another T-shirt?" Sharon asked. "One without paint on it?" Sharon realized she must sound like she was Tiffany's mom. Tiffany was both streetwise and naive, and Sharon sometimes felt protective of her young employee. She'd snatched Tiffany away from their former workplace because she was quick to learn and naturally talented at hairstyling skills.

"Brought one along," Tiffany said, picking up the tote bag she'd left in the corner that morning. "By the way, Tom has a cousin he'd like to fix up with someone—maybe for a double date. His cousin is about your age, and—"

"No."

"I know," Tiffany said with patience as she pulled out the extra shirt. "You're steering clear of relationships right now. But—"

"It's called celibacy."

"Okay, I understand." Tiffany tilted her head to one side. "Sort of. But this would just be for dinner out somewhere, the four of us. No big thing."

"Sometimes 'no big thing' can lead to a *great big thing* that takes over your life. What if I meet Tom's cousin and *like* him? Then what? Just say *no* if he asks me out again?" Sharon shook her head and exhaled. "I know myself, Tiff. When it comes to men, I can't always get my willpower in gear. I made a commitment to myself, and I'm sticking to it—no men to tangle up my life and distract me from my goal until my salon is running successfully for... at least a year."

"Another *year?*" Tiffany's eyes widened with a combination of amazement and disappointment, but she accepted Sharon's answer. "You sure have more willpower than I'll ever have—or want," she muttered under her breath as she zipped up the tote bag. "I'll go change in the rest room and then I'm off. See you tomorrow."

When Tiffany was gone, Sharon silently commended herself for making the right decision. Her goal was to make Wanna Be's *the* place for hair care in Orange County, and nothing was going to sidetrack her from her chosen path. Men often had a way of restructuring a woman's priorities, she'd learned from experience. When Sharon met a man she really liked, her first priority always became keeping him happy. When she was working with Tiffany as a stylist at their former employer's, Sharon would often rearrange her work schedule to suit the current man in her life, so her hours would conform better to his work hours. That enabled her to spend more time with her boyfriend, but sometimes it also meant that she earned less income than she might have otherwise. She liked men a little too much, she'd finally realized.

Sharon knew that her strong point, the thing she had going for her now, was that she'd identified her own foibles and she was doing something about them. She had learned to control her temper, which used to be as fiery and unmanageable as her hair. Her search for inner serenity through well-practiced methods of relaxation and self-control had also helped her to wean herself from the compulsive need to have a man around. Her road to success, she'd decided, would be paved with peace of mind, sexual celibacy and a total focus on her goal of starting her own business.

So far, it was working very, very well. All lights were go. Success was just ahead. She could feel it, sense it, as if she had ESP. Despite her occasional doubts, she still felt in the depths of her very centered self that something great was about to happen.

Early the next morning she handed an envelope with her ad and a hefty personal check to QWIN's portly, thirtyish, ad salesman, who seemed to have a constant sunny disposition. "Thank you," Rick said, looking pleased as he slipped the envelope into his briefcase. "We always appreciate new accounts. I'll give your commercial to Stoney. You've listened to his show, haven't you?"

Sharon made a patient little smile. "No."

"No?" Rick's hazel eyes began to lose their sunshine, as if a feeling of foreboding was clouding his optimism. "Oh." As he closed the lock on his briefcase, he sighed with resignation and mumbled, "Déjà vu all over again."

"Stoney, do me a favor and be gentle with this one?" Rick had scribbled on a yellow self-adhesive note. It was stuck to the typed ad Stoney Ross found waiting for him at the station at four forty-five Monday morning. His show began at five o'clock.

"Tough luck, Rick," Stoney muttered as he crumpled the yellow note and tossed it into the wastebasket. He read through the ad, chuckled and jotted a few notes in the margins.

Later, at a few minutes after eight that morning, the ad and other papers and computer printouts lay in front of him in the cluttered, glass-enclosed QWIN broadcast studio. After sipping hot coffee, Stoney adjusted his headphones as he waited for the latest Meat Loaf song to end. He did not glance at the Wanna Be's ad now, even though he was about to do the commercial on the air. He'd always been noted for his uncanny ability to read copy cold, and too much familiarity kept him from being fresh. He worked best by feeding his raw ideas directly to his mouth. This allowed his famed irreverence to flow before his internal censor had time to stop him from saying things he shouldn't.

His trademark spontaneity had put him at the top of Top 40 radio in the U.S. by age twenty-five. He'd recently turned thirty, celebrating two years as "Top Jock" at QWIN radio—this, after a successful three-year stint at WLS in Chicago, a tough radio market in a tough town, where he'd honed his style. He was still riding high. He ought to be happy about so much success in such a precarious industry, but somehow, lately, he wasn't.

Turning thirty, despite the raucous all-night party thrown for him a few months ago by his friends, had made him think about his life. Something or other seemed to be missing, only he couldn't figure out what. It had begun to bother him so much, he'd taken up smoking again—a habit many disc jockeys seemed to have, but one he'd been proud to have kicked over a year ago.

As the Meat Loaf tape drew to a close, Stoney resisted the impulse to light up. His producer, Harve, a young man with brown hair and a beard, came in and sat in the chair next to him again. He'd left the studio briefly to get more coffee. Harve assisted Stoney in working the board, the array of buttons and switches laid out in front of them to which all the equipment, from the microphones to the tape players, were connected. An aspiring disc jockey himself, Harve also served as the morning show's newscaster and weatherman.

Harve checked the stopwatch around his neck to anticipate the moment the song ended, then pressed a button to turn on Stoney's microphone.

"That was the latest from Meat Loaf," Stoney said over the air. "You're listening to the Top Jock, Stoney Ross, on QWIN Radio here in pristine Orange County, where we feel sorry for all you folks breathing the noxious vapors up in L.A. Traffic report in a minute. Gotta hear a commercial first—that's the deal."

He riffled quickly through the papers in front of him, which seemed to have shifted. Harve rushed to his assistance.

"Here it is," Stoney said, hiding his discomfiture beneath his glib on-the-air voice. He began to read "'Everyone wants to be at Wanna Be's, Newport Beach's hot new styling salon at Fashion Island.'" Stoney snickered. "Well, if it's so *hot,* try installing some air-conditioning."

He resumed reading. "'During Wanna Be's Grand Opening this week, all services will be twenty percent off...' What a deal! 'Everything from perms, foil weaves...'" He paused at a new idea, his memory clicking, brain whirring. Then he chuckled wickedly. "I'll tell you about a personal experience I had with foil weaves in a minute," he told his listeners in a sly, intimate tone, then continued, "'... tints and cuts, manicures, complete make-overs, facials, even aromatherapy.'"

Pause. "What's aromatherapy? You sniff a daffodil instead of seeing a shrink? 'Complimentary coffee, tea cakes and wine will be served ...' Oh, I get it. The aromatherapy is when they make you smell coffee to revive you after all the wine and tea cakes—and the hot air!"

He laughed, slapping his palm on the desk, enjoying his own joke. "This sounds like quite a salon! If they start offering massages, I'll be there! '... so make an appointment now to pamper yourself under the care of Wanna Be's expert staff. Call Sharon at 714 555-3131 today, and—'" his eyes speeding ahead, he chuckled "'—begin to be all you want to be at Wanna Be's.' Whoa! Testing the Top Jock with a tongue twister, Sharon? It'll take more than wine and tea cakes to make Stoney Ross blow a line. Try again, sister!"

* * *

At that moment in Newport Beach, in the cubbyhole office of Wanna Be's, Sharon listened to her radio, her mouth open from shock. "I don't believe this!"

"Now don't get upset," Tiffany said, putting a hand on Sharon's shoulder.

"Shh!"

Stoney's distinctive and, to Sharon, unpleasant voice, a gruff, sardonic monotone, came from the radio again. "Let me tell you about my experience with those...um...what are they?" The rustling of papers could be heard. "Foil weaves. I had this girlfriend a while back—a hotty, natch. I only settle for the best in babes. By the way, you ladies out there can stop writing me all those letters inviting me for dinner and whatnot. I'm very selective. *Highly* selective. I mean, get real. I'm not going to call you up for a date because you write and tell me you make a great beef Stroganoff. I have higher specifications than that—like measurements, and I don't mean just height and weight. I look over women with the same precision as I look over cars, and I like a good pair of headlights, you know? Keep sending the interesting photos, though." His subtle chuckle had a suggestive edge.

"But back to my former girlfriend. She had a hair appointment and she asked me to pick her up afterward. I got to the salon on time, but they were running late. When I saw her, I nearly went into cardiac arrest. She had layers of tin foil sticking straight up out of her hair in all directions."

Sharon and Tiffany exchanged horrified glances as someone else, another man, could be heard laughing in the background.

Stoney said, "I'm not kidding. You think I'm making this up? Little sheets of aluminum growing out of her head! It was then that I realized the truth about her. She obviously was an alien from another planet. I asked her why she hadn't told me her secret, 'cause, you know, we'd become pretty cozy. She tried to tell me it was one of those foil weaves, but, hey, I wasn't buying her story. I flew out of there so fast, they probably thought I was Superman. Never saw her again!''

The other man was still laughing, and Stoney started chuckling himself. ''So,'' he said in a concluding manner, ''if you want to know where all those aliens from outer space are—you know, the ones who land on the UFOs that you read about in the tabloids—check out your local beauty salon. They're all probably gathering at Wanna Be's even as I speak!''

Absolutely furious, Sharon could hardly speak. She felt blood rushing to her temples and heat coming out her ears. ''That…that…*maniac* is going to get his! He won't know up from down when I get through with him!''

Tiffany looked a shade paler. She turned down the radio's volume, then tried to restrain Sharon from reaching for the phone by grabbing her arm. ''No, Sharon. Don't call the station. Give yourself a chance to calm down first.''

''I don't want to calm down!'' Sharon exclaimed, wrenching her arm out of Tiffany's grasp. ''I'm not *going* to calm down until that motor mouth is six feet under!'' She pushed around the papers on her desk, looking for the business card Rick Slocum had given her. ''Where's that phone number!''

Tiffany reached around her and swiftly picked up a small card off a corner of the desk.

''Is that it?'' Sharon asked, too blind with rage to see straight. ''What are you doing? Give it to me!''

''Not until you calm down,'' Tiffany said with a slightly shaky voice, holding the card behind her, as if determined to keep her ground in the midst of an exploding volcano.

"Tiffany Lindstrom—"

"I'm doing this for your sake," Tiffany insisted. "I was afraid this would happen. You won't do yourself or Wanna Be's any good if you let loose your temper on anyone but me. Why don't you try some alternate nostril breathing?"

"The only breathing I'm going to do is blow fire down Stoney Ross's throat! Now give me that number, Tiff, if you value your life!"

"Sharon, please—"

"Tiffany—"

Pressing her lips together, Tiffany relented and gave her the card.

Instantly Sharon was on the phone, dialing the number. When the QWIN receptionist answered, she demanded to speak to Stoney Ross.

"He's on the air and can't be disturbed," the receptionist said. "Can I connect you with anyone else?"

"Rick Slocum," Sharon said, tight-lipped with impatience.

"Just a moment."

In seconds an affable low voice said, "Slocum. May I help you?"

"Yes. You can string up Stoney Ross by his thumbs and leave him for the vultures!"

"M-may I ask who this is?"

"Sharon Harper at Wanna Be's. Did you hear the way he read my commercial?!"

"Yeah, I...I did." He laughed nervously. "That's Stoney for you. New sponsors often have this reaction, if they aren't familiar with his style. You'll get accustomed to it."

"*Accustomed?* Are you out of your mind? He's made my salon the laughingstock of Southern California. He's ruined my business before it's even started!"

"Wait a while and see what reaction you get from the public. You may be pleasantly surprised."

Sharon could see she would get nowhere with this fork-tongued Pollyanna. It was his job to find unsuspecting new sponsors for his station, so what could she expect? "I want to speak to Stoney Ross this instant!"

"I'm sorry, you can't do that, Ms. Harper," Rick told her with a beleaguered exhale.

"Why not?"

"Stoney has ironclad clauses in his contract that he can't be disturbed during his show and that he is not required to talk to sponsors at any time."

"What recourse does a sponsor have, may I ask? Other than demanding that you take my ad off the air and asking for my money back."

"Now, now, give it a chance, Ms. Harper. I'll bet you get lots of customers calling just from today's commercial. Stoney may have had some fun with it, but I bet everyone listening will remember Wanna Be's from now on."

"Fun with it?" Sharon shot back. "He ridiculed my salon, called it a hangout for space aliens! He insulted all women who *go* to salons. He even made a snipe at *me* and called me 'sister'!" Sharon's mouth could hardly keep pace with her spiraling anger. "So he won't talk to his sponsors, eh? Well, you tell him that if *this* sponsor ever gets her hands on him, Mr. Top Jock Numbnuts will be walking funny and talking two octaves higher!" With that she slammed down the phone.

"Oh, no, Sharon," Tiffany moaned, sitting down limply on an extra chair in the room.

Sharon sat in her swivel chair, recovering, catching her breath. The room was silent for a full minute except for the low sound of rock music coming from the turned-down radio.

All at once Sharon slid low in her chair and said to Tiffany, "Well, what do you think? Did I make a total idiot of myself on the phone?"

"I'm afraid you did."

Sharon shook her head with dismay. "I haven't gone ballistic like that in years."

"It's not that I blame you," Tiffany sympathized. "He often jokes about the commercials, but I never heard him go that far before. I'm sorry. I feel like this is my fault. I suggested his show."

"Well, it *is* the top show. It made sense. I should have taken your advice and listened to him first. Now, instead of handling this like a professional businesswoman, I chewed out that salesman like a fishwife."

"Maybe you should call him back and... well, apologize," Tiffany suggested.

"I should apologize for my anger," Sharon agreed, straightening up in her chair. "But I had a right to complain. How does Stoney Ross keep his sponsors if that's the way he treats them?"

Tiffany lifted her shoulders, as if not knowing how to reply.

All at once the phone rang. Sharon looked at her coworker. "Will you answer it? Maybe it's Rick calling back trying to make amends. I'm not sure I'm ready to talk to him yet."

Tiffany quickly rose from her chair and picked up the phone. "Hello, Wanna Be's."

Sharon was surprised to see her reach for the salon's appointment book.

"Sure. We have most of the afternoon open. What time would you like to come?" After writing a notation in the appointment book, Tiffany hung up. "It's a customer. She said she heard about us on the radio."

Sharon felt odd, taken off guard by the unexpected. "I guess Stoney Ross put us on the map, all right," she said, unsure whether to be happy or remain upset.

Tiffany went out of the office to open up the salon. Sharon's radio had a tape player, so she inserted an Enya tape, closed her eyes and listened to the soothing, uplifting music for about fifteen minutes. After a few more minutes of breathing exercises, her pulse was calm and she felt in control of herself. She dialed the QWIN phone number again and asked for Rick Slocum.

When he answered, she made a polite apology for the way she had spoken earlier. Then she said, "For the moment, I've decided not to take my ad off the air. But would you please see to it that from now on Stoney Ross merely reads my commercial as I wrote it, with no embellishments of his own?"

Rick was silent for a second. His voice was hesitant and flat as he replied, "Of course, I'll tell him. But . . . well, to be frank, Ms. Harper, Stoney doesn't tend to take . . . um . . . guidance from anyone. Since Stoney came to this station, it's been one big roller-coaster ride."

Sharon was beginning to feel sorry for Rick, having to work with such a manic, male prima donna. "I can imagine. Thanks for being frank and for being patient with me. But you understand that I have to look out for my interests here. If Stoney messes with my commercial again, I'm *off* the roller coaster. Got it?"

"I'll do what I can, Ms. Harper."

"Thanks." As she hung up, she had the feeling Rick probably couldn't do much of anything. Apparently Stoney Ross was a sacred cow at the station, because of the ratings he pulled in.

In a moment, she had to resume her alternate nostril breathing to calm herself again. She'd become over-energized at the thought of tanning Stoney Ross's sacred hide.

2

The next morning in Wanna Be's office, Sharon turned on her radio again with trepidation. Tiffany came in to listen, too. Stoney Ross sounded exactly the same—brash, rude and irritating. Sharon couldn't understand why anyone would want to begin their day listening to his raw voice and abrasive manner. And his comments yesterday about women were downright chauvinistic.

"I've got a letter here from Judy, who's thirteen," Stoney was saying. "She writes that she listens to my show every day while she gets ready for school. Good for her. My show is a great way for a young girl to put herself in the right frame of mind for science and math and literature." There was distant laughter in the studio. Sharon wondered who was with him as he did his broadcast. She also began to be curious about what the smart-aleck disc jockey looked like.

Stoney chuckled, and then for a moment the radio seemed dead. All at once his voice cut in again. "Anyway, she writes a nice letter. Boring, but nice. I'll just read you the question she wants to ask me. 'Stoney, if all the women are after you that you claim are after you, then why don't you get married? You always say you're allergic to marriage, but I know that's just one of your jokes, because marriage isn't something a person can be allergic to, and if you were a married man, the women who chase you that you complain

about wouldn't chase you anymore because you'd be un
available, right?' "

Stoney seemed to take a moment to consider the ques
tion. "I was never a whiz in English class, but I believe
you've got a run-on sentence here, Judy. Better ask your
teacher about that before your next test. As for your opin
ion about my allergy to marriage, I don't care what science
may say. I *am* allergic to marriage. I know most people are
allergic to pollen, dust, cat hair, and other airborne stuff. Or
you can be allergic to foods, too. I also know that marriage
is a legal relationship and you can't breathe it or eat it. But
I swear to you on a stack of Bibles that whenever a female
starts hinting to me about marriage, I have an allergic re
action. I break out in hives, or I get a sneezing fit. Once I got
the hiccups for three days. Now, some might say my reac
tion is all psychological." He snickered with derision.
"Well, I don't buy that. *No way.* You think I'm afraid of
commitment or something? Of course not! Top Jock is
afraid of nothing. I'm committed to my show, right? I'm
committed to the Angels baseball team, am I not? I'm
committed to freedom, the red, white and blue, and the
good old U.S. of A. I'm not *afraid* of commitment! I'm just
allergic to marriage, that's all. End of subject."

The loud crinkling of paper could be heard, as if he were
crunching the letter into a ball near the microphone.
"Bull's-eye into the round file with that one. Time for a
commercial. Gag me with a service, it's Wanna Be's again."

Sharon stopped breathing and her jaw tightened as she
listened. She glanced at Tiffany. If he dared—

"Let me give you an example of what I have to put up
with from sponsors," Stoney went on. "This one . . . what's
her face . . . Sharon Harper, who runs Wanna Be's, had the
nerve to call and complain about the way I, Top Jock, the
numero uno DJ in the country, read her commercial yester

day. Said I should read it as she wrote it with no embellishments. Not only that, she used language unbecoming a lady! Rick, our poor salesman, a man who would apologize to a mosquito before swatting it, took her call. He was pink with embarrassment when he repeated what she said. You know what she called me? Cover the ears of any young children who might be in earshot. Ready? Mr. Top Jock Numbnuts. Sharon Harper called *me* Numbnuts.''

Distant laughter came from the nether-reaches of the studio and now Stoney was laughing, too. Sharon looked helplessly at Tiffany, who had covered her face with her hands.

"I have to admit," Stoney continued, "it's kind of clever. But I was *shocked*," he insisted, new drama in his voice. "Simply shocked. And then, she threatened me. Something to the effect that I'd walk funny and talk with a high voice if she ever got her hands on me. Well, don't worry, Sharry baby, you'll never get your hands *there*. I wear iron jockstraps just to protect myself from tough cookies like you. I tell you, men, it's a new world out there. Women used to be demure and sweet. We used to have to open doors for them, because they were so helpless. Now look at them. You go on a date with a woman, you'd better wear armor. And you want to know why I'm not married!''

Sharon felt the heat of humiliation and anger rise to her face. He was making her the laughingstock of half the state of California!

"Just to show how I try to satisfy my sponsors, I will now present Sharon's commercial the way she expects." In a voice surprisingly smooth and pleasant, he read her ad exactly the way she wrote it, taking on the manner of a typical announcer. When he finished, his voice suddenly became raucous. "Now that you're all asleep, I'll wake you up!''

Instantly the harsh sounds of a heavy-metal band jarred the room, and Sharon reached to lower the radio's volume.

Abruptly the music stopped. She turned the sound up again as Stoney proclaimed, "No one tells Stoney Ross how to read a commercial. The eagle does not take flying lessons from the turkey. If you don't like my style, buy time on another station, lady!"

Livid at the personal attack directed at her on the air, Sharon flicked off the radio and reached for the phone. Tiffany instantly clamped her hands down on Sharon's wrist and arm.

"No, Sharon! Don't make the same mistake twice," Tiffany pleaded. "He'll only come back at you again tomorrow."

Sharon let go of the phone and banged both her fists on the desktop. "Damn him! How can he get away with this? I'd sue the jerk, if I had the money for a lawyer." She slumped in her chair and looked at Tiffany. "You're right. If I complain again, he'll only insult me again. He controls the airwaves, so he'll always have the last laugh." She chewed her coral-tipped fingernails. "I could cancel the commercial for the rest of the week and demand my money back."

"But, Sharon, we got dozens of calls yesterday for appointments, and most of them had heard about us from his show."

"I know. It's not fair! He's making my salon successful at *my* expense."

"Well, success is success. After the things he said today, we may get a new bunch of women customers just out of female backlash to his male backlash."

Sharon looked up. "I hadn't thought of that." She rubbed her upper lip nervously. "Oh, okay, I'll leave well enough alone. But I feel that I've been publicly insulted and there's nothing I can do about it. I may practice to be calm and rational, but there's still a scrappy part of my personality that craves revenge.''

"I know," Tiffany soothed. "I don't blame you. But I don't think there's any way to get it. And revenge is a negative goal."

"You're right. Absolutely right. It's not good for my peace of mind to even think about it," Sharon said, to herself as much as to her friend. She could feel her pulse racing, like a horse at the starting gate, and she knew her temper was barely tethered. But it would take more than alternate nostril breathing to get over this.

Stoney Ross was just too powerful, too self-important and egotistical—and too damn rude. *Somebody* ought to take him down a notch *somehow,* she silently fumed. Boy, did she wish *she* could be the one.

Stoney Ross was leaving the broadcast studio when he was approached by his boss, the production director.

"I want to see you and Rick in my office," Al Albright said. "Now."

Stoney followed Al down the hall, silently exhaling with fatigue and resignation. He'd been through these impromptu little meetings many times before. While Al stopped to get coffee from the coffeemaker at the end of the short hall, Stoney walked into Al's office. Rick was already sitting at a small, round conference table. The salesman also looked tired, his tie askew, his forehead reddened from his habit of rubbing it. He lifted two fingers in a mock salute.

Stoney lowered his lanky body into the chair next to Rick and asked, "What gives?"

"I think it's about the Wanna Be's commercial."

Stoney nodded, having suspected that. "Did she call again and complain?"

"Not yet," Rick said ominously. "But yesterday she threatened to cancel. Maybe she's calling her lawyer. I asked you not to mess with that one. Can't you take a hint? Sharon Harper never listened to your show before."

"Never heard my show," Stoney replied in a deadpan. "Is she deaf? Doesn't speak English? Just moved here from the South Pole?"

Rick seemed annoyed. "Stoney, will you give it a rest? You're not on the air, now. If you'd just followed my advice, we wouldn't be here waiting to get the ax from Al."

"He won't give you the ax. It's not your fault."

Al came in with a cup of coffee, closed the office door and sat down at the table with them. Al was pushing forty, losing his brown hair and gaining weight around the middle. He wore a blue sports shirt and gray cotton pants.

Al locked Stoney with his gaze, something not many could do. "What is it with you? Since you came to QWIN, I've had to go back on Prozac. After this morning, I'll need to double my dose!"

Stoney thought it wise not to reply.

"Where was your common sense today when you did the Wanna Be's commercial?" Al demanded.

"I never claimed to have any," Stoney said matter-of-factly.

"Don't you learn from experience? Ms. Harper threatened to cancel yesterday. Most DJ's might say to themselves, well, the sponsor is upset, I'd better be careful next time. But you? No, you go in the next day and wipe up the floor with her."

Stoney spread his hands outward. "I thought she was egging me on."

"Egging you on?" Al repeated, his dark eyebrows closing together like twin thunderclouds over his nose.

''She called me Numbnuts. If that's not inviting a counterattack, I don't know what is!''

Rick covered his eyes with his hand. ''God, I wish I'd never told you what she said.''

Stoney turned to Rick. ''You said she *demanded* that you deliver her message—'Tell Mr. Top Jock Numbnuts that if I get my hands on him he'll be walking funny and talking an octave higher.'''

''Two octaves,'' Rick corrected, lowering his hand from his face.

''Two?'' Stoney jerked his head back as if hit with a punch. He looked at Al. ''See what I mean? I figured she's egging me on, deliberately looking for a fight.''

Al shook his head incredulously. ''I think you're the only one in the world who would interpret it that way. From what Rick said, she was steaming mad.''

''Scalding,'' Rick agreed.

''When people are that angry, they say things,'' Al continued. ''And she had a right to be mad. She'd expected you to just read her commercial, not make a comedy routine out of it.''

''I make the commercials part of the entertainment,'' Stoney said, annoyed that he had to explain and defend his style yet again to his boss. ''Or else, no one would pay attention to them. I can't help it if some sponsors don't understand that I'm doing them a favor. Rick said she never listened to my show before. It's her own ignorance that got her into trouble.''

''Even if that's true,'' Al argued, ''did you have to rip her to shreds on the air today and tell her to buy time on another station?''

''If she's not satisfied, she should take her business elsewhere,'' Stoney said. ''Isn't that common sense?''

"Stoney," Al said with a show of great patience, "you can't outright insult the people who buy ads on your show. They're the ones who keep our station out of the red. They're the ones who pay your astronomic salary!"

Now Stoney really began to get perturbed. "Look, you lured me away from Chicago with that astronomic salary exactly because of my brash style. You can't have me both ways—I'm not schizophrenic! I can't do my show with one personality and then switch and do the commercials with another. If it's a problem, then why don't you take only pretaped commercials? Then all I'd have to do is play them."

Al looked as if he was trying to calm himself by smoothing back the graying hairs above his ear. "Not all sponsors can afford or even want a prepackaged commercial. I'm proud of the fact that our station is one of the few that still gives sponsors options." Al's voice began to rise again. "I'm not changing QWIN's policies for a disc jockey who admits he has no common sense. You could at least *try* to filter and edit what you say about our sponsors before you say it!"

"That's not how I work!" Stoney shot back. "If I start censoring myself I'll sound just like every other bland jock on the air."

"You're right," Al said in a deceptively quelled tone, "and that's why I've let you off the hook until now. But you've gone too far with this one. If Ms. Harper cancels, I'm holding you personally responsible."

"According to my contract," Stoney said, "I am not required—"

"I don't care about your high-falutin' contract!" Al exclaimed, rising from his chair, his face growing red, the veins in his neck protruding. "If she cancels, you're in major trouble!"

"Remember your nerves, Al," Stoney said, growing concerned. "Cool down."

Al sat down and seemed to deliberately lower his voice. "I'm in control, and I'm warning you—"

"Okay, okay," Stoney said, putting up his hand, palm out. "But what's done is done. What do you expect me to do about it now? I can't pull back what I said out of the airwaves."

"You could apologize to her," Rick said.

Stoney shot him an *are you crazy?* look. "She hasn't called to cancel yet, has she?"

"No," Rick said.

"Well, maybe she's seen the light. Maybe she won't cancel."

"Stoney," Al said in a booming voice. "You're not weaseling out of this."

"But it's her move," Stoney insisted. "Shouldn't we wait to see what she does?"

"No!" both men said at once.

Stoney glanced from Al's stern face to Rick's. "What, you want me to phone her? Or go to her salon bearing flowers and gifts?"

"That sounds good," Al said.

"Wanna Be's just opened," Rick interjected, "so flowers would be a nice Grand Opening gift."

Stoney couldn't believe what he was hearing. "Look, I'll go to the salon and talk to the babe, but there's no way I'm bringing her flowers. You want her to have flowers, *you* call a florist and have them sent. And you'd better sign the card QWIN Radio. I don't want my name on it."

"But you'll go to Wanna Be's and see her?" Al asked.

Stoney eyed his boss, trying to ascertain whether there was any way he could get around this. Al's bloodshot, searing eyes told him there wasn't. "Yeah, okay, I'll go over there and talk to the chick."

"Don't call her a chick or a babe, Stoney," Al said. "She's a sponsor. You call her Ms. Harper and you do it with respect."

"Right," Stoney said. "Of course."

"And what are you going to say to her?" Al asked.

Stoney shook his head. "Beats me. I'll decide that when I see her."

"Stoney, this isn't a situation you handle off-the-cuff," Al told him. "You ought to have something in mind to say to her."

"Like what?" Stoney asked.

Al exhaled in an exasperated manner. "Rick's suggestion about an apology was a good one."

His stomach beginning to turn with distaste, Stoney pointed his forefinger at his boss. "Look, I'll do what I can. But you can't make me go where my mouth won't take me!"

3

———◂———

That afternoon, while leaving the station, Stoney had to dodge the persistent female groupies who apparently had nothing better to do than hang out in the parking lot to get a glimpse of him and pester him for autographs. Getting past them to his car, he drove off and had lunch by himself at his favorite restaurant.

He stewed over his California burger and then puffed a cigarette, which left a bad taste in his mouth. Stoney decided he was as ready as he'd ever be to meet and try to smooth things over with his new nemesis, Sharon Harper.

He'd decided not to call before going over to Wanna Be's, figuring he'd have the advantage if he took her by surprise. If he had to say so himself, he usually made a good initial impression on women. People often fawned over him, once they learned he was a celebrity. He'd probably have sharp-tongued Sharon eating out of his hand by the end of the day.

He drove to Fashion Island, a huge, upper echelon, outdoor shopping mall in Newport Beach surrounded by a broad, circular driveway. Eventually he found Wanna Be's, a small salon next to a popular health-food restaurant.

Stoney walked through the glass door and noticed there was no one behind the reception desk. But inside, behind a decorative lattice partition, he saw a couple of hairdressers, a blonde and a redhead, and three women customers, one under a dryer, one getting a shampoo and one having her hair cut. The blonde finishing the shampoo put a towel around her client's hair and came up to him, while the redhead giving the haircut, whose back was to him, went on snipping.

He wondered which one was Sharon Harper.

The attractive blonde wore denim shorts and a tight knit top calculated to show off her full, high breasts. She had a body to die for, but Stoney also noticed the oblivious gaze of youth in her eyes—a lack of life experience that quickly made him lose interest. *I must really be getting old,* he thought, surprised at himself. In any case, she certainly didn't strike him as the potentially treacherous type. He couldn't tell about the slim redhead in the short leather skirt, however.

"Do you have an appointment today?" the blonde asked, looking a little puzzled. "If not, it's okay. We can squeeze you in."

"I'd like to see Sharon Harper," Stoney replied, beginning to feel ill at ease. Being a barbershop sort of guy, he was uncomfortable in a salon with women customers. And he didn't like his purpose for being there in the first place.

The blonde walked over and whispered to the redhead, who finished another snip, then turned around. Her bright green eyes connected with his across the room in a frank, friendly, unblinking stare. "I'm almost done with my client," she told him. "Be with you in a minute. Have a seat." She turned back to her customer.

Feeling peculiarly dumbfounded, Stoney nodded and sat down on a vinyl seat near the reception desk, to which the blonde had gone to answer the phone. *That's Sharon Harper?* he thought, glancing again at the redhead. She had a quick, graceful little body and a fine-boned, enchanting face. Her thick wavy hair was held back with a gold clip on one side in an asymmetrical style that he imagined few women could wear, yet it gave her the appearance of a cover model. Her slender legs looked sensational as she moved back and forth in her high heels, blowing her customer's hair dry.

He found himself remembering one of the female characters in the musical *Cats*. He'd seen a road tour of the show at the Orange County Performing Arts Center a few years ago. The part of Rumpleteazer was played by a slim little sprite, a delightful dancer who had more energy than anyone he'd ever seen—until now.

As he watched, Sharon turned off the dryer when she'd finished and walked around to face her customer. The gray-haired lady apparently said something amusing, and both laughed. Sharon's wide, ready grin showed lots of teeth and a lively sense of humor.

Stoney felt an odd, sinking feeling in the pit of his stomach. She had the most genuine smile he'd ever seen. She appeared to be just what he liked and seldom found: an authentic young woman with quick enthusiasm and a fun-loving nature. He found it hard to believe this was the same spitfire who had chewed out Rick Slocum so mightily.

Stoney began to grow nervous—an unusual state for him. But he felt at a loss, somehow. He didn't know how to handle this, how to accomplish his purpose and not embarrass himself in the process. He straightened his back and tried to remind himself who he was. Stoney Ross was supposed to be cool—at least he always claimed to be to his audience. But how could he maintain his famous cool while making amends to this uniquely beautiful woman?

Can it, Stoney, he instructed himself as the gray-haired lady got up to leave and Sharon began walking toward him. *She's just another babe. So she's a stunner. Get over it!*

"Here for a cut?" Sharon asked. Before he could answer, she reached out and started fingering his hair. She ruffled it first this way and then the other, apparently to see how it fell or maybe to get an idea of its texture. She did this without a hint of shyness. In fact, her manner was quite businesslike. Yet, her unexpected playing with his hair was at once so gentle and tantalizing, it gave him pleasant goose bumps. He was sorry when she abruptly stopped.

"Well, you need a new cut, all right," she told him in the authoritative manner his doctor used to advise him to eat a healthier diet and stop smoking. "This style is five years out-of-date. Come over to the sink." She pointed to a row of sinks with chairs in front of them, where he'd seen the blonde giving someone a shampoo.

An electric sensation sped through his body as he realized what she meant. *She's going to wash my hair.* He reeled inside just slightly, his mind blown. But he only hesitated half a second, remembering and then shoving aside his reason for coming here. There was no way he was going to pass this up!

Sharon was slightly startled to see the man's gray blue eyes widen when she motioned toward the sink. She supposed he was one of those men who only went to barbershops, where they cut hair dry. But he readily stood up to follow her, so she stopped worrying about it. His height surprised her—he must have been a full foot taller than she. He had a great head of hair, too—naturally wheat blond, darker at the nape, with a strong, silky texture. Robert Redford had nothing over this fellow. His angular jaw, narrow straight nose and silvery inquisitive eyes were equally striking. With the cut she had in mind for him, she'd have him looking like a movie star when she was finished.

He sat down in one of the reclining chairs in front of a sink, looking a bit awkward. She smiled to herself as he seemed surprised again when she put cellophane over his denim shirt collar and wrapped white towels around his neck. She wondered what he did for a living. If he *were* a movie star, he wouldn't be so diffident about getting his hair washed. He'd be used to it. Maybe he was a construction worker as her father had been. She wondered what had made him decide to come to a salon.

"What's all this for?" he finally asked when she draped a blue, water-resistant shampoo cape over him.

"Keeps you neat," she said.

"I don't mind getting a little wet."

The comment made her chuckle. He really was kind of sweet. If she wasn't careful, she'd wind up hoping he'd come back on a regular basis. It wasn't that she didn't need more regular customers—she did. But she didn't want any distractions. This guy was going to be a dilemma for her, she had the feeling. Well, maybe he was married. She hoped so. But she glanced at his left hand as he brought it out from beneath the cape, and he wore no wedding ring. Not all men wear them, she reminded herself. She ended the back-and-forth argument she was carrying on in her mind by deciding that a man as handsome as he was *must* be married.

"Lean back," she told him, and started the water running.

Stoney had always assumed that the concept of paradise was pure mythology. As Sharon leaned over him and slowly massaged fragrant soap into his hair with her gentle, sensual fingers, he decided Wanna Be's must *be* paradise, or as close as he'd ever come to it. He'd give her an hour to stop. But to his disappointment, it didn't last nearly that long.

"Water temperature okay?" she asked as she started to rinse.

"Fine." He was afraid it was almost over, but then she massaged more soap into his hair, starting the process all over again. Closing his eyes, he gave himself over to her tender touch, glad the telltale bulge beneath his zipper was covered by the cape she'd put on him.

"What's your name?" she asked.

"Sto—" he began, then caught himself, quickly coming back to his senses. No, he just couldn't make himself tell her who he was. Not *now;* not when he'd do anything to keep her doing what she was doing to him. Maybe in a while, when she wasn't hovering over him this way, her feminine fingers in his hair, her top giving him marvelous glimpses of the inner curves of her breasts. "Stanton," he told her, using his true given name, a name that only his mother in Cleveland used anymore.

"Stanton?" she said, turning on the rinse water again. "That's an unusual name. Do people call you Stan?"

"Some have," he replied. It was true. Back in grade school, most kids called him Stan until his best friend started calling him Stoney, because he used to collect rocks and fossils. Soon everyone but his mother called him Stoney, and it stuck.

He felt deprived when she brought out a towel to dry his hair and asked him to sit up again. He'd have eagerly sat through a dozen more shampoos. He'd love to take her home with him and have her give him a leisurely bath. A vision of her in a big tub with him, submerged in luxuriant soap bubbles, washing every part of his body with her sensitive hands made his zipper feel tight again. What was the matter with him? He had to remember who she was, who he was, and why he was here. He'd better start thinking about cold showers instead.

She directed him to a large, upholstered swivel chair in front of a big wall mirror. He sat down, the cape still draped over his front, ending just above his knees. As she combed out his wet hair, she asked, "What's your last name?"

"Perossier." Again he gave his real name, not his professional one.

"Gosh, that's a mouthful."

"I know," he murmured, silently chiding himself for still keeping his identity hidden. He'd have to tell her about his other, public, identity sometime today, before he left. He'd promised his boss to make peace with her for roasting her commercial. But she was so pleasant to be with, to have fussing over him, he hated to take the chance of spoiling it all. She was liable to have a hissy fit the instant he told her. He'd have to wait until the right moment came along.

All at once, an alternative plan occurred to him. He could simply tell his boss that he'd met Sharon and that they'd gotten along well. It would be true, strictly speaking. But, of course, it would be misleading and he might get found out in the end, if Sharon decided to cancel her ad. Maybe he could get a feel for what her intentions were regarding the ad.

"I heard about this place on the radio," he said innocently as she carefully took a small, very precise-looking pair of scissors out of a black leather case. She set them on the counter in front of him and picked up her comb again.

"Stoney Ross's show?" she said. Her green eyes seemed to have little incandescent flames in them now. "Do you believe that guy? The nerve! I'd like to—"

Suddenly the blonde piped up from across the room. "Sharon, don't get started."

Sharon seemed to catch herself. She nodded. "You're right, Tiffany. Thanks."

"Don't get started on what?" Stoney asked with feigned ingenuousness.

"I tend to get my dander up talking about him. Tiffany's reminding me not to, so I don't get all worked up again."

"You were angry?" he urged.

"You heard the way he did my commercial, didn't you? He made fun of my shop, then when I complained, he ridiculed *me*. And I paid a lot of money for that! I couldn't believe it. The man's an egotistical maniac."

"Sharon," Tiffany chided her again.

"He wanted to know," Sharon explained to her co-worker. As she said this, she combed and recombed a lock of Stoney's hair at the top back of his head, her hands moving with quick, angry strokes.

"Why don't you take your commercial off the show and ask for your money back?" Stoney asked, looking at her in the mirror, for she was standing in back of him.

Sharon stopped working, leaving his lock of hair sticking up, the ends drooping, and tossed the comb onto the counter. She walked around to his side, so she could look at him directly. "You've hit the problem on the head," she said, placing her fists on her narrow hips. "He's done my commercial only twice and it's already brought me more customers than I ever imagined. We've gotten lots more phone calls today and we're booked up for a month already. We're also getting walk-ins like you."

Stoney blinked. He hadn't realized he was a "walk-in."

"We don't even have our whole staff yet," Sharon went on. "A receptionist, a manicurist and a cosmetician all start next week. And if we keep getting customers at this rate, we'll have to take on another hairdresser pretty soon. I'd never anticipated my business would get off to such a fast start. I'm smart enough not to argue with success, so I'm not canceling my radio ad. But, boy, would I like to get

Stoney Ross in a back alley someday." Her emerald eyes flashed as she said this.

Stoney found himself incredibly turned on by her sparkling energy, her spunky temper. This was one hot chick. Her threat about getting him in a back alley amused him. He couldn't resist saying something. "I can see you're angry, but be careful. You're a little too small and slender to take on a man," he pointed out with a chuckle.

Sharon tilted her head as she looked at him, her long hair falling in a new pattern around her shoulders. Then she picked up the sharp scissors she'd left on the counter. "You see these?" she asked with a smile, holding them up in her delicate hand. "They're made in Germany of the very finest steel. I may not be big, but I'm skilled enough to use these on him and clip off whatever I think ought to go."

Stoney had no reply. He sat speechless as she picked up the comb again, went back to the same lock of his hair and with great precision, began snipping. Her scissors were so fine and sharp, they made no sound as she worked. He felt little cuttings of his own hair fall onto his shoulders, and his hands instinctively moved beneath the shampoo cape to protect the most vulnerable part of his anatomy. He could understand now how she might have thought up the term Numbnuts.

He decided it would be wise not to bait her anymore. Changing the subject, he asked, "Have you always been a hairdresser?"

"After graduating from high school, I went to beauty school, and then I went to work in a salon. Never had any other job."

"And now you own your own salon," Stoney commented. "I didn't realize hairdressers made that much money."

She laughed, her genuine grin reappearing. "We don't. I inherited enough money to start my own business, along with some help from a bank."

"Inherited?" he asked, curious. Did she come from a wealthy family?

"My dad was a construction worker. He made pretty good money and always believed in saving for the future." Her smile faded. "He died last year of cancer. He was fifty-one. I was an only child, and he left me his life savings." She lifted her shoulders in a sad, poignant way. "I'd rather still have him with me than have the money. After my mother died when I was a teenager, he and I became very close—more so than most fathers and daughters, I think. He was always very supportive of me. Just before he died, the last thing he said was that I should take the money and start my own salon, as I'd dreamed of doing. He wanted that for me. So..."

She stopped speaking, pressed her lips together in a little smile and went on cutting his hair in silence. As Stoney studied her face in the mirror, he realized she'd grown too emotional to continue talking. And suddenly he felt like a heel, having publicly made fun of her salon on his show, when it meant so much to her. He really wanted to apologize now, not because his boss told him to, but because he felt he should. But if he did, he'd have to tell her *he* was the rude disc jockey who had insulted and provoked her. Somehow, he didn't want to do that while she still had the scissors in her hand.

"What do you do?" she asked, disturbing his train of thought.

"Huh? Oh, I'm...in communications."

She looked puzzled as she combed through his hair, apparently checking to see if she'd missed a stray strand. "Is that like telephones and fax machines? Computers?"

"Um, I'm more in media communications."

She made a half smile. "I'm afraid I don't know much about those things. That's why I'm beginning to regret that I never went on to college. I started this salon, but I still don't know all I ought to know about running a business—you know, accounting, marketing, supervising people, all that stuff."

Stoney found himself disarmed by her honesty. He'd never finished college, either, but he usually kept that to himself. "You seem to be doing just fine. But you can still take business classes at a local college and learn what you need to know. I'm starting a management class next week, for example."

Her eyes brightened and she stared at him in the mirror. "You are? But I thought you already knew business."

Stoney lowered his gaze, then looked up at her again. "I quit college after two years. I've been taking some classes after work to eventually get my degree."

"No kidding," she said, eyes bright and questioning. She appeared so interested that she seemed distracted as she put down the scissors and picked up the hair dryer. "I've thought of taking college classes to learn business, but...I guess I'm afraid to. I wasn't much of a student in high school." She chuckled. "I was one of those girls who only thought about hair, makeup and boys."

Stoney grinned. "I was into music and bands. The neat thing about going back to school when you're older is that you pay attention because you want to learn. You've finally realized you need the education to insure your future. I've made much better grades at the college classes I've been taking than I ever did when I was in high school. You may surprise yourself."

The shining lights in her eyes took his breath away. She looked so hopeful and excited. Instead of using the hair dryer in her hand, she rested it a moment on his shoulder and asked him in the mirror, "What college do you go to? Is it too late to sign up? Could I take the class you're taking? I'd feel better if I knew someone else in the class."

Stoney told her which local college he went to and said that if the class wasn't full, he believed she could still register. "I'd be happy to see you in class with me," he found himself adding.

Her expression changed slightly, becoming self-conscious apparently, as he looked at her in the mirror. She lifted the hair dryer from his shoulder, as if just now aware of what she was doing. "I . . . I don't mean . . . I mean I just want to be friends. You know, talk about the teacher and compare class notes. I'm not . . . Your wife doesn't need to worry about me latching on to you, is what I'm trying to say," she explained with an embarrassed grin.

Stoney stared up at her face above his in the mirror. "I'm not married."

"Oh. Well, then your girlfriend doesn't have to worry."

He didn't have a current girlfriend, either, but he refrained from confessing that. "So," he deduced, "you're single, too?"

"Single and very happy that way," Sharon replied. "I've got too much on my mind to think about any kind of relationship right now."

She started up the hair dryer then, so Stoney couldn't make any further comment. Not that he had one to make. The fact that she wasn't interested in a relationship bothered him. Women nowadays were so self-sufficient, it seemed they could take men or leave them. As a man, Stoney didn't like the idea of being totally unnecessary in a woman's life. Especially if he was beginning to like the woman.

Well, when he spilled the beans about who he was, she'd never go out with him anyway, so...

A new idea dawned in his mind as hot air from the dryer rushed past his ear. *So why tell her?* he asked himself. That could wait. He'd found out she wasn't going to cancel her ad, so he was out of danger with his boss. He could wait until they got to know each other more, till she understood all the different aspects of his personality. Over time, there would come some ideal moment when he would tell her the truth. And maybe she would accept it. Maybe by then she wouldn't hate Stoney Ross anymore, either. This was a much better plan, he decided.

She shut off the hair dryer, gave his hair a final comb through, then took off the cape. When he looked at himself in the mirror, he had to admit he was impressed. He ought to be on the cover of *GQ,* he thought. He'd never looked *this* good in his life.

"What do you think?" she asked, holding up a hand mirror so he could see how it was cut in the back.

"Looks great," he said.

"I took it up over the ears," she explained, "because it accents your cheekbones better, and I think the length on top is good for you. And it's current, as far as style."

He smiled at the deliberation she'd put into it. He'd never thought much about his hair and considered haircuts a nuisance, which explained why his hair usually got overgrown and shaggy. He'd never look at a haircut the same way again. "You're an expert," he told her, swiveling in his chair to look at her directly. "I'll be happy to recommend Wanna Be's to everyone."

She looked a little mystified. "I'm glad you like it. You sound like you know a lot of people."

"I *am* in communications," he said, trying for a joke. He found himself growing nervous again. "Would you like to have dinner with me sometime? Tonight maybe? Or tomorrow night?'' The invitation spilled out of him as his heart rate increased. He wanted her to say yes, even though she'd already indicated she wasn't looking for a relationship. Stoney Ross, the Top Jock, wasn't used to being turned down by women; but, to Sharon, he was Stanton Perossier, a nice ordinary guy who had only himself to offer, not fame and fortune. Her answer to Stanton meant more to him than he wanted to admit.

As he held his breath, Sharon lowered her eyes and appeared taken off guard and confused. After a moment her eyes met his, and she gave him that smile that stirred his heart and turned his mind to butter. ''Thank you, Stan, but I'll have to say no.'' She had the grace to look downright wistful, while little lights played in her eyes. ''You're much too attractive, and I'm staying on the straight and narrow right now, to be sure Wanna Be's is a success. But I'll probably see you in that class.''

He thought it must be the prettiest refusal any guy had ever received. He made a little shrug and nodded his head. ''See you in class.''

A few minutes later, as he walked down the street toward his parked car, his head was spinning. Sharon was unique. He'd never met anyone like her. She was a woman with a life and a purpose, and she knew what she wanted and when— much the way he'd been all through his twenties, when he was moving from city to city and climbing his way to the top of Top 40 radio. His gut feeling told him that she was the woman he hadn't known he was waiting for.

Unfortunately *he* was the man she didn't know she hated.

4

The next morning at Wanna Be's, Sharon tuned in QWIN on a new radio connected to the salon's speaker system that Tom, Tiffany's boyfriend, had installed for them the night before. A Rod Stewart song was playing. She intended to change to her usual New Age station once Stoney Ross read her commercial. Feeling edgy, she wondered what he would have to say about it or about her today.

The salon wasn't open yet, and Tiffany had said she was going to be late because of a dentist appointment. While the radio played, Sharon got the coffeemaker going and readied the hot water for tea. She also put cookies and scones, picked up at a local bakery, on a tray and set them out for customers.

That done, she took a large, colorful flower arrangement off the high counter at the reception desk and brought it over to one of the sinks to add water. The flowers had arrived late yesterday afternoon with a Grand Opening congratulatory note signed, "The QWIN Staff." Surprised, Sharon had assumed it was a form of apology from the radio station, probably sent by Rick Slocum. As she carried it back to the reception desk, she wondered if Stoney Ross had been reprimanded and if so, if it would affect his manner today.

The music had stopped, and he was reading another letter from a kid, this time a ten-year-old boy named Tommy. Stoney read the letter in his characteristic cynical, ultramale low voice. His voice was a paradox—curiously flat and unexpressive, yet it sharply communicated his irreverent view of the world.

"'What are your favorite foods? Do you eat vegetables, or do you hate them like I do?' Well, that's a really important question, Tommy, and I'm glad you asked. The health-food aficionados say that we are what we eat, right? So, let me think about this. My favorite meat is hamburger—no, make that cheeseburger. My favorite dairy food is coffee ice cream with nuts. When it comes to fruit, I like strawberry margaritas. As for veggies, of course I eat them! I want to be healthy and strong, don't I? My favorite vegetable is green jelly beans—but only those that are picked fresh."

Sharon surprised herself. She was actually chuckling at his jokes. Too bad he couldn't show this gentle sort of humor more often. Her smile disappeared, however, when he announced, "Time for a Wanna Be's commercial." She stopped wiping up drops of water left on the counter from the flowers and listened, her muscles tightening with trepidation.

"Yesterday I told Sharon Harper, the salon's owner, to take her commercial on down the road if she didn't like my style. Alert listeners will remember me revealing the shocking fact that she'd phoned the station and called me 'Numbnuts.' I properly pointed out that it wasn't a very ladylike term. Well, we haven't heard another word from the lady, so I have no choice but to risk reading her commercial again. But I tell you, I've...I've learned my lesson. I can't have our staff or our audience exposed to such brazen language, so she won't catch *me* messing with her message again."

He proceeded to read her commercial in a straightforward manner, not with a smooth-talking announcer's voice, but with his own sarcastic edge. He added no needling asides or personal interjections, however. When he had finished, he said, "By the way, I know someone who actually went down to Wanna Be's after hearing about it on my show. This…let's say it's a close friend," he said suggestively, "a *really* close friend, told me Sharon Harper gives an expert haircut. Said she was swift and sassy with a pair of scissors."

There was a momentary pause, no sound coming over the radio. Sharon stood motionless, listening, then was startled when his cocky voice suddenly returned. "But then, I could have predicted that. Stands to reason. Any hairdresser with a comeback attack as sharp as hers would have the scissors to match. Ol' Numbnuts here will keep his distance, thank you, but the rest of you go on down to Wanna Be's. Sharon will whip you into shape before you know what hit you."

Sharon leaned against the counter and shook her head, feeling mystified. Since he didn't massacre the commercial itself this time, she surmised that he truly must have been reprimanded by his superiors and had taken heed. But he still seemed to have it in for her.

She couldn't help but wonder who the close friend was— his current girlfriend apparently—who had come in to get her hair styled. It might have been any of a dozen new female customers who were attractive enough, since Stoney had made it clear he had high standards. Which one had it been? she wondered, trying to remember and picture the various young women who were new clients. She was curious about what type of woman would actually attach herself to someone like him. But she couldn't recall anyone saying they knew him.

A rock song was playing as she thought about these things, but Sharon didn't change the station. She decided to listen to his show some more. In a perverse way, he *was* sort of fascinating, she had to admit. What would he say next? That was the question that kept everyone listening.

Two current hits played and then a recorded commercial for a car dealership came on. Finally Stoney's voice was on the air again.

"'Sorrowful Joe's Restaurant in Costa Mesa is now open for breakfast, as well as lunch and dinner.' Great! I wonder if his eggs are as greasy as his burgers."

Sharon's mouth dropped open. Stoney was reading someone else's commercial, and he was ridiculing that one, too! Didn't he learn? She was certain he'd get a complaint from the irate restaurant owner, just as she had complained about her commercial. What was the matter with him?

"'Belgian waffles, pancakes in ten delicious flavors'—like what, chocolate and vanilla? You know, to a chocoholic, vanilla is a joke, not a flavor. Oh, wait, he names the flavors here—sorry, should have read ahead faster." Distant laughter came from the background. "Top Jock's losing his edge!" Stoney said, laughing. "Let's see, he's got 'banana pancakes, peach, strawberry, coconut, chocolate chip...' See? I was right after all. 'Peanut butter...' You've got to be kidding. 'Buttermilk...' It's getting worse! 'And other sensational flavors. Sorrowful Joe's also has eggs any way you want along with your choice of bacon, sausage, hash browns and grits.' Grits? Does Joe realize he's in Southern California, not South Carolina? Out here you have millet, oat bran, or sprouts. It might not go with eggs, but that's what they'll put on your plate. 'For a hearty breakfast and a great cup of coffee, start your day right at Sorrowful Joe's on Bristol near MacArthur. Open at 6:00 a.m.' Sorry, Sorrowful, that's not early enough for me. I'm up at four-thirty and I eat breakfast on the air at five. Which explains why I have trouble giving the call letters at that hour. It's hard to say QWIN with a mouthful of powdered doughnut. Yeah, it's rough," he said with a tone of self-pity, "but I do it for you, my faithful audience. Where would you all be if you didn't have me to shake you awake every morning? Now— what? Oh, the weather. My bud, Harve, is here with an update on the forecast."

Another male voice came on that Sharon hadn't heard before, probably because she'd never listened to the show long enough. Tiffany came in then.

"How did it go at the dentist?" Sharon asked her.

"No cavities, but I had a crack in one filling. What did Stoney say?"

"He read the commercial okay, but he saved a few jabs for me. Did any of your customers mention that they knew Stoney Ross?"

Tiffany's blond eyebrows drew together. "You mean, personally? No."

"He said a close friend of his came in here and had her hair done. I've been trying to figure out who it was."

"Really?" Tiffany said, eyes brightening. "Was she his girlfriend?"

"I'm assuming it was."

"Wow! Stoney Ross's *girlfriend* was here at Wanna Be's! I wonder which of us did her hair."

As the disc jockey's comments on the radio played through her mind, Sharon remembered. "I think he said that *I* gave the haircut, and he was actually complimentary about it. But then he went into a little diatribe about how somebody as sharp-tongued as me would have sharp scissors, too."

Tiffany's face lost some of its wonder. "So he got nasty again?"

"Sort of. Not as bad as yesterday. But later," Sharon said, her voice tightening as her temper began to surface, "he read a commercial for a restaurant, and he made mincemeat out of that. I don't understand how he gets away with it! That's what really irritates me—he's a jerk who makes his living being a jerk. Maybe his show's a success, but it's at the expense of other people—his sponsors."

"Now, Sharon—"

"Right, I know. But he just gets to me. How must that poor restaurant owner feel?" She paused, staring into space as a thought came to her. "You know what? I think I'll call that restaurant and see what he says. Maybe if the people who advertise on QWIN get together, we can do something about Stoney Ross."

Tiffany seemed hesitant. "You think that's wise?"

"It can't hurt to ask," Sharon said, going behind the reception desk to pick up the phone book. She found the number for Sorrowful Joe's and dialed. When she got the owner on the line, Joe Smejkal, she introduced herself and told him about her experience with her radio commercials for Wanna Be's. "I really don't know what to do, because Stoney controls the airwaves," she lamented. "When I heard what he did to your commercial this morning, I couldn't help but sympathize. So I thought I'd call and see what you think about it."

"What do you mean, sympathize?" the growling voice replied. He sounded like an older man. "I thought Stoney was great!"

Sharon was dumbfounded. "But...he said your hamburgers were greasy. He made fun of the pancakes."

"Look, sweetie, Stoney eats lunch here at least once a week. Sometimes dinner, too. He's my best customer. Got his autographed photo up on the wall. I've been advertising on his show ever since he came to QWIN, and I've got

more customers than I can handle most days. So don't
bother me with any more sympathy, honey. I ain't got the
time."

"Sorry. 'Bye." Stunned, Sharon hung up the phone, then,
hand on her hip, turned to Tiffany. "Is the whole world going nuts, or is it me?"

"What'd he say?"

"He *likes* the way Stoney does his commercials. Stoney
even eats lunch at his restaurant. They've got his picture on
the wall!"

As if no longer able to keep a straight face, Tiffany suddenly broke out in laughter. "I love it! You're just not with
it, Sharon. Maybe the New Age music has numbed your
brain. Better get on the bandwagon."

"Would you like to leave here tonight alive?" Sharon
said, playfully reaching out as if to wring Tiffany's neck.

Tiffany backed away, still laughing. "I don't mean to
tease you. But you haven't listened to Stoney enough yet to
realize that no one takes him seriously. It's just his nutty
sense of humor, and everyone takes it with a grain of salt."

Sharon shrugged in exasperation. "Apparently I'm not
nutty enough to appreciate him. I'll try harder."

"This salon means a lot to you," Tiffany said, her tone
empathetic now, "and it's hard to see things from a neutral
point of view, like his listeners do."

Sharon nodded. "Maybe." She still didn't think, however, that while lampooning a commercial he needed to
personally insult the person who bought the airtime. For
example, he'd panned Sorrowful Joe's burgers, but he
hadn't made a public fool of Joe himself. Maybe it meant
she needed to work more on her sense of humor, but she
couldn't help but feel personally attacked, not once, but
twice, on the air to a potential audience of millions. A small,
persistent voice inside her continued to call out for revenge,

and she seemed unable to silence it. She was beginning to truly hate Stoney Ross, because he made her feel so helpless and ineffectual. If she could just find some way to chalk up a point against *him* for a change! The fact that he'd toned down his reading of her commercial wasn't enough. He still spoke with prickly disdain about her. Who did he think he was? More than ever, he needed a dressing-down, and she continued to wish she could find some way to accomplish the task.

A while later, after their first customer had come in, Stoney read another letter on the air. This one was from an adult, a woman, and he read it with what sounded like a sense of respect.

"Dear Stoney Ross, I listen to your show as I drive to work, and I really enjoy it. However, I do have a bone to pick with you. You're very popular with children and adolescents, yet you've mentioned now and then that you smoke. Certainly it's not my place to tell you what to do in your personal life. But you might refrain from mentioning on the air that you smoke, as it sets a bad example for the young people who admire you. Just a thought from a concerned mother of three. Yvonne Brimmer."

"You're absolutely right, Yvonne," Sharon was surprised to hear Stoney say when he'd finished reading. "It's not my intention to advertise my bad habits, but since I let my mouth run free while I'm on the air, sometimes it slips out. A couple of years ago, I smoked so much that I got a hacking cough, which didn't sound too pleasant over the radio. I managed to quit. Did it cold turkey, too. But, a few months ago I started again for no good reason. I'm trying to limit myself to five cigarettes a day, and I hope to quit again entirely. Your point about my younger listeners is well-taken. So, I've got a bulletin for you kids out there—I may be the Top Jock and a really cool dude, but you'd be even cooler than me if you don't pick up my bad habit. Don't smoke! End of message."

A rock song came on then, shaking Sharon's concentration. Tiffany, who was assisting her with a foil weave on their customer, seemed to take notice.

"Want me to switch it to a New Age station?" Tiffany asked. "You look like you're getting tense."

Sharon hadn't realized her demeanor. "Yeah, why don't you? Thanks."

Tiffany walked to the equipment set up in a corner and in a moment the gentle soothing sound of a pan flute floated through the room. As Sharon worked on her customer, she felt herself relax a bit at the change in music, but her mind was still active. Tiffany returned to assist her and began a conversation with the real estate agent whose hair they were highlighting. Sharon was glad to let Tiffany entertain the woman, because she couldn't pull her thoughts away from Stoney Ross.

She'd been surprised at his serious reply to Yvonne's letter. Yvonne had managed to make him own up to his behavior, had made him act responsibly. Her accomplishment seemed almost miraculous, given his personality. Sharon wondered if there was some way she could do the same, regarding his treatment of his sponsors. If Sharon wrote him a letter, would it make a difference?

Probably not, if she signed it. It would only add fuel to their running feud, and he'd most likely use it as an excuse to insult her on the air again.

But what if Sharon pretended to be someone else, another listener, writing him? He might take the letter more seriously, as he had Yvonne's. He might take stock of him-

self, as he had with the letter about smoking, and change hi
behavior. It seemed worth a try.

But how? What name would she invent? What ton
should she take? What should she say to him, exactly? She
realized that she'd have to make her letter brief and inter
esting, or he might never read it and comment—and tha
was what she wanted, for him to read her rebuke on the ai
and then make a public apology. A long, boring letter woul
be pushed aside, because he'd be most concerned abou
keeping his audience entertained. The more she though
about it, the more of a challenge composing such a lette
became. Well, she'd managed to write her own commercial, so why not give this a try? There was nothing to lose.

When she drove home that night to the Santa Ana hous
she'd grown up in, the letter to Stoney remained foremost o
her mind. She tried to relax by reading the newspaper in he
living room, sitting in the recliner her father always used, a
a Yanni tape played on her stereo. She read an advice col
umn and a health column written by a doctor. Then she
came to her favorite column about modern-day etiquette. A
she enjoyed the popular columnist's proper but sprightly
style, Sharon began to form an idea of the tone and ap
proach she might use in her letter. Stoney Ross might have
had provocation to give back what he got from Sharon
Harper, who had chewed him out with ill-chosen language
But how would he react to a classy lady who was simply too
highbrow to insult?

Putting the paper aside, she went to her bedroom and
found some flowered stationery given to her by an aunt. She
got a pen, sat down at the kitchen table and began writing
When she'd finished, she considered what name to invent to
sign the letter. Maybe one name was enough. What about
her middle name? she wondered, biting the end of the pen
She never used it, never even told anyone what it was, be-

cause it had always sounded old-fashioned and odd. But for the new persona she'd created in her letter, it seemed perfect.

Using sweeping strokes of her pen, as graceful as she could make them, she signed the letter "Ione."

It was Friday, the end of a long week, and Stoney looked forward to the weekend, which for him began when his morning show was over at 10:00 a.m. But that golden moment was more than five hours away and he had a show to do. As he read through mail addressed to him that had arrived at the station yesterday after he'd left, he put aside a few letters that were good enough to read on his show.

Harve checked the letters Stoney had selected. "What order do you want to read them?" The bearded young man kept the computer printout of the day's selection of songs, the written commercials, the news and weather reports and miscellaneous articles and papers in order, since Stoney tended to misplace things when he was on the air.

Stoney sorted the letters in his mind. "Let's start with the letter from Ione after the news at six. She sounds like the type who'd be bright-eyed and bushy-tailed at that hour."

Harve looked at the letter written on expensive feminine stationery. "She's bringing up a touchy subject. What are you going to say? You'd better be careful, with Al monitoring your show so closely."

Stoney took the letter from him and studied the large, unusually graceful penmanship. "I think I've got Al off my back for now. I told him I saw Sharon Harper, that she gave me this haircut and she decided not to withdraw her commercial." He of course had left out a few pertinent details. Al had bought his version of the truth, however. "Besides, I think I have a good way to deal with this letter."

When Harve finished reading the news at 6:05, Stoney picked up the flowered sheet of stationery. "Got a letter here from someone named Ione. I don't know if you pronounce the *E* on the end or not. Isn't that a subatomic particle or something? No, that's *ion*. Anyway, this is what she says. 'My Dear Mr. Ross...' Now, see, I like that. *Mr.* Ross. Shows respect."

"I must admit that I am a new listener to your show. I also confess that I am quite ignorant of current fashion and custom on rock-and-roll radio stations, such as QWIN. Perhaps you can shed light on an issue that perplexes me.

"When a gentleman or gentlewoman buys airtime, as I believe one says in the broadcast world, to advertise their business on your show, are the inventive heckles you add to their commercials gratuitous? Or do you tack on an additional fee for the extra time you take to insult your sponsors? When you verbally assaulted poor Ms. Harper of Wanna Be's and poor Mr. Sorrowful of Sorrowful Joe's, for example, did you send them revised bills? Or were each given the opportunity to deduct the cost of their slaughtered commercial from your salary, to which their advertising fees must contribute?

"I look forward to your kind response to my humble questions. Sincerely, Ione."

He was silent for a long moment while Harve sat nearby, nervously stroking his beard.

"I'm not sure what to make of this letter," Stoney said at last, adjusting the microphone in front of him. "I must be attracting a new type of listener. I've got to admit that Ione writes a damn fine letter, though. It's like being punched in the gut with a satin-covered boxing glove. Listen to the high-class vocabulary, here—gentleman and gentlewoman, gratuitous, kind response. She sounds like that woman in the papers who writes that etiquette column. Except you might look up the word *humble* in the dictionary, Ione. 'Cause I don't think your questions could be described as humble. I mean, you're asking about deductions from my salary—not exactly a meek inquiry.''

Harve started laughing, and Stoney couldn't help but chuckle, too. ''Well, listen, Ione. You're obviously upset about the way I read commercials, though I'm not sure why. Tell you what I'll do. I'll answer your question, to the best of my humble ability, but first I need to know more about you. A gentlewoman such as yourself must understand that a gentleman like me wouldn't answer personal questions like that to someone I don't know. Write back and tell me more about yourself. Like, do you have a last name? And how about your age? I'm talking ballpark. Under forty or over? I know a lady doesn't ordinarily discuss her age, but I need some demographics on you if you expect a reply. And most of all I'd like to know why the hell you wrote me this letter. On flowered stationery yet. What's it to you, my *dear* lady, if I 'slaughter' somebody's commercial?'' He took the letter in his hand and crumpled it into a ball next to the microphone. ''No answers, Ione, until I get some answers from *you!*''

Stoney pressed a button on the board in front of him, and a Janet Jackson song began. He turned off the microphone and glanced at Harve. ''Guess I told *her!*''

Harve nodded. ''What if she's some little white-haired grandma in a rocking chair? Hope you didn't give her a heart attack.''

Stoney opened Ione's crumpled letter and studied it again. ''Her handwriting's too smooth for her to be elderly.''

"Why do you want her to write again? She's asking you a messy question."

Stoney lowered his voice and leaned toward Harve. "You think maybe Al secretly wrote it, to teach me a lesson?"

Harve laughed. "That thought occurred to me, too. But Al writes cramped and backhanded. He couldn't match Ione's writing on a bet. He wouldn't use language like that, either."

"No," Stoney agreed. "Nobody uses language like this, not for real. She seems to be having a go at me, and I'd like to find out who she is and what her motive is."

"Motive?" Harve repeated humorously, eyebrows raised. "Sounds like you think she's planning to murder you."

Stoney cocked his chin to one side. "Beneath the lacy language, there *is* a hint of venom. That's just it, I don't know why she's got an ax to grind." As he studied the uncrumpled letter, a new thought came to him. "Unless she's flirting with me."

"Flirting!"

"She's deliberately picking a fight with me. Some women do that to get attention. Instead of sending me a photo of herself naked or inviting me to dinner, she's taking me on. She even hides her identity to add mystery to herself. It's an unusual tack and shows some ingenuity. I've responded on the air, so she's gotten her reward. Bet it won't take her long to write again."

"If that's true, then she might be one of those crazies who'll wind up stalking you and going through your garbage."

Stoney hadn't thought of that. "You must have a morbid bent of mind today! I don't think so. She sounds too intelligent. She's not like the groupies who lie in wait for me in the parking lot. I think she's either somebody who truly dislikes my radio personality and wants to get it off her chest, *or* . . . she's someone who's secretly attracted to me. Maybe she doesn't even know why, because she thinks I'm raw and irreverent. So she writes in this classy tone to put herself above me, but she's really flirting with me. For her, it's like playing with fire.''

"You sure you aren't letting your groupies, your ratings and your fan mail go to your head?'' Harve asked, a let's-get-down-to-earth look in his eyes. "You're reading a whole lot into a letter. She might be seventy years old. She may feel she's made her point and never write you again."

Stoney gave him a challenging stare. "How much you want to bet? I say she's under thirty-five. And she'll write within three days. Hundred bucks?''

"On *my* salary? How about a burger at Sorrowful's?''

At home, still in her bathrobe, Sharon paced the floor. She had switched off the radio, since the music jarred her already-ruffled composure. How had her letter backfired? Why hadn't he taken her questions seriously and responded seriously, the way he had to Yvonne, the listener who had written him about his smoking?

She remembered Yvonne had signed her full name and written a short, straightforward letter, with no attitude or artificiality. Stoney must have sensed Ione was playing games with him rather than just stating her point as Yvonne had done. And now he wanted Ione to write back, so he could verbally spar with her some more. Damn! Why hadn't she signed it Ione Smith and just written to him in an ordinary manner? Why did she have to tease and taunt him?

On the other hand, with the way Sharon felt toward him, how could she have written a letter that didn't taunt him? No matter what format or personality she invented, the taunt would have still shown up in her letter one way or another. She wasn't trying to protect youth like Yvonne.

Sharon had a personal ax to grind! She might as well admit it.

So, now what? Should she write again? What purpose would it serve? He'd just outmaneuver her once more. She'd said her piece. His audience had heard her complaint. Why not be satisfied with that?

Sharon paced the length of the kitchen again. She wasn't satisfied. She still wanted to score at least one little point against him, win one battle over him, if not the war. He was so smug, so egotistical, so cavalier about his sponsors! Even if he got the better of her, at least her point was still being made. Sensible people in his audience would see that Ione had some valid objections to raise. There was some justice in that, Sharon told herself.

Okay, yes, she'd write another letter—why not? Ione had only a brief life to live before she was buried for good; and before she bit the dust, she had more to say to the world on the subject of QWIN's swell-headed Top Jock!

Sharon got out the flowered stationery she'd used before and sat down at the table. After a few minutes of thought, she began writing.

Two days later, Sharon's clock radio woke her at 6:00 a.m. She'd reset the radio to QWIN, so as not to miss Ione's letter, if Stoney chose to read it. It ought to have arrived yesterday.

Sure enough, after the news, Stoney announced he'd received another letter from Ione. Sitting on the edge of her bed, Sharon bit her lip as she listened to him read in his grating monotone.

"My Dear Mr. Ross,
Thank you for reading my letter, though you failed to respond to my inquiry about your treatment of your

sponsors. Instead you asked me questions of a personal nature, claiming you needed answers before you could give me answers. I find your logic spurious, but I will humor you.

"About my age...I consider myself ageless in mind, spirit and truth. In body I may well be younger in years than you, though you are certainly the younger in maturity.

"As for my name...of course I have a surname, but I am a private person and wish to preserve anonymity.

"As for my purpose in writing you, I felt morally burdened to speak up. Perhaps your long-suffering sponsors are too intimidated by your ferocious manner to protest your treatment of them. My sense of justice was aroused. So, in the role of an innocent bystander, who by happenstance has begun listening to your show, I took it upon myself to raise pertinent questions on their behalf.

"Now, dear Mr. Ross, I believe I have given the answers you required of me. Please be so kind as to reply to my questions, as you promised. Sincerely, Ione."

Sharon stiffened with nerves, her hands fidgeting. He'd read the letter straight through without comment. She wondered what bomb he was waiting to drop this time.

"You're quite a piece of work, Ione!" he exclaimed over the radio. "I'm more confused by your answers than enlightened. Why all this fancy talk and beating about the bush? You say you're probably younger than me. Then why not just state your age? Seems like that would be more *mature* than all your hokum about mind, spirit and truth. With your screwball logic, I can understand why you don't want people to know who you are!

"Now about this 'morally burdened' business. Did my sponsors *ask* you to get all 'morally burdened' on their behalf? And this 'innocent bystander' thing—like you were there just minding your own business, and my commercials happened to you? Did you get into some accident listening to me read one?"

He chuckled in a suggestive manner. "Unless by 'innocent' you mean virginal or something. Is that it? You lost your innocence listening to me do a commercial? Man, I wish I could have been there! You must really get intense when you hear my voice. Of course, that's not so unusual—I do have that effect on women."

Over her radio, Sharon heard laughter in the background and then a loud thud, as if someone had slapped a hand on a desk. "Yeah, I see now what this is all about. You listened to me have my way with one of the commercials, and it felt like a ride to the moon, eh? Look, lady, I'm not responsible for any moments of ecstasy you females may sustain while hearing my voice. Listen to me at your own risk. I accept no responsibility!"

Stoney was laughing now, sounding as if he was genuinely enjoying himself. Sharon, however, was fuming. The man had no boundaries, no respect, no sense of crossing any lines!

"Well, look, Ione, since this has become such an issue for you, maybe I can help you work this through. Why don't you write again? Bare your soul. Tell me all about yourself. Actually you must be one hot chick, to have such an erotic reaction. No wonder you say here that your sense of justice was 'aroused.' I should've noticed that before! Was it a Freudian slip? Or did you purposely say that to give me a hint about what's *really* on your mind? I'm on to you now, Ione, you highbrow vixen you. Write me again—this is better than phone sex!"

Loud rock music blared then, and Sharon switched off the radio with an angry jerk. The nerve! How could he twist her words around that way? Thank God she'd decided to keep her name a secret. She should have guessed someone with his mentality would turn everything into sexual innuendo. And he still hadn't answered her!

So he wanted her to write to him again, did he? Well, Ol' Numbnuts would have a long wait!

5

After finding the correct building on the small college campus, Sharon walked down the hall looking for the room where the Business Management class she'd registered for was located. It was early evening and she'd eaten a quick homemade sandwich at Wanna Be's before leaving for class. She found Room 104 and walked in, feeling a little self-conscious and tentative. It had been years since she'd been in a schoolroom of any kind.

As soon as she walked through the door, one of the dozen other students already seated started waving to attract her attention. She smiled with relief mixed with excitement when she recognized Stan Perossier. He stood up and motioned for her to sit in the empty student's desk in front of him.

Sharon walked to the desk. "Hi, Stan. How are you? You look great!" It was an understatement. He was still sublimely tall and looked so handsome with his new haircut and crisp oxford shirt, she knew she'd have trouble concentrating all through the class.

"So do you!" he said, his silvery blue eyes glistening at her. "I was hoping you would register for the class. Any problems?"

"No. There was room, so they took me." She sat in front of him and twisted in her seat to talk to him as he sat down again.

"How's the haircut? Any problem handling it?"

"No. It's fine."

She couldn't resist reaching out to touch his hair. He readily leaned forward so she wouldn't have to stretch. Ruffling her fingers through the thick blond strands, she mussed it just slightly and made it come down a bit over his forehead. "There, now it looks sexy. If I only had some hair spray."

His grin appeared, then he laughed. "Thanks, but I'll pass on the hair spray."

To Sharon's embarrassment, she realized that some of the other students, male and female, were watching them with curiosity. "I'm his hairdresser," she explained to them.

"Wanna Be's at Fashion Island," Stan added.

The students watching smiled and, one by one, turned their heads forward again.

"I'd better be careful," she told him in a whisper. "I don't want to embarrass myself the first day of class."

"The instructor hasn't come in yet," he reassured her. "You're safe."

"I'm nervous," she confided, getting a pen and note-book out of her purse.

He shrugged, an elegant movement on his slim, broad-shouldered, long-boned frame. "It's just a class. No big deal."

"I haven't bought the textbook yet, have you?"

"No. We can go after class to the bookstore and pick them up."

"You know where it is?" she asked.

"Sure."

The instructor walked in then. Sharon turned forward in her seat and attempted to look studious. When the class began on the hour, the instructor, a man of about sixty with wavy white hair, took roll call. Sharon couldn't help but smile to herself when he stumbled pronouncing Stan's last name, Perossier.

After class ended, Sharon walked across campus with Stan to the bookstore. Along the way she asked a few questions about the college. Eventually he asked how business was going at Wanna Be's.

"Better than I ever expected," Sharon replied. "We've got more clients than we can handle and we're taking on another stylist."

"Guess your commercial on Stoney Ross's show did the trick then," he commented.

"I have to admit it did."

"So, you like him now?"

Sharon had to laugh. "Are you kidding? He's the most egotistical, self-serving Neanderthal I ever encountered."

Stan's pace slowed. "Wait a minute. Neanderthal?"

"He's got that caveman mentality. He thinks with his zipper."

Stan seemed surprised and smiled. "He does?"

Sharon was beginning to wish she hadn't gotten into this conversation with a man, but she might as well explain her point. Stan must be more sensitive than Stoney—*any* man had to be.

"Are you up early?" she asked. "Did you hear the way he responded to that letter from Ione this morning?"

Stan nodded. "I heard him read it."

"He read it, and then he turned her words all around and made them into sexual innuendos. She was trying to make a serious point, and he made out that she... she..."

"Had the hots for him?"

Sharon sighed. "I suppose that's the way he would put it."

"Maybe she does."

Sharon stopped and turned on him. "Oh, come on! Not you, too."

He put up his hands. "Look, I agree that Ione's trying to make a point. She's pretty priggish about it, too. But he's got a show to do, and if she sasses him, he just uses the opportunity to sass her back. It's just for entertainment, that's all."

What did he mean, priggish? she wondered. "And I suppose messing up my commercials was just entertainment, too?"

"Toward the end of the week, he read your commercials without making fun of them. In fact, on Friday, for your final commercial, he even said, 'See you at Wanna Be's,' as if he was planning to go there himself."

Sharon nodded. "I'm not holding my breath. I thought that was odd, because earlier he'd said Ol' Numbnuts wouldn't go near the place."

Stan hesitated. "I don't think he put it quite that absolutely. By the way, did you really call him that?"

Sharon could have bitten her tongue, wishing she hadn't repeated the word in front of Stan. "I'm afraid I did. I don't normally talk that way, but I was so angry, I didn't think."

"It's pretty funny. Did you make it up?"

She chuckled. "My father used to say that, joking with his friends while they played poker once a week. You know how men rib each other. That's where I heard it."

They arrived at the bookstore and came back out several minutes later with their purchased class textbooks.

"How about some coffee?" Stan asked. "There's a cafeteria here." He pointed to the small building next to the bookstore.

Sharon thought it over for a second. She really didn't want to start anything resembling a dating situation with him. But on the other hand, he'd been friendly and supportive toward her on her first day of class, and she didn't want to seem standoffish. The truth was, she really liked him. Why couldn't she have met him next year, instead of now, when she had to give her full attention to Wanna Be's?

"Okay," she said, "just a quick cup."

They entered the cafeteria and got their coffee, but he waved away her dollar when she took one out of her purse. *What's one little cup of coffee?* she thought to herself. *Why argue?*

They sat down at a small table together, opposite each other.

"You still look nervous," he observed. "Class is over."

She studied the steam coming out of her cup, then looked up. "I guess I'm nervous around you."

"Why?"

She hesitated, then decided to go ahead and say it. "Because I like you. And I have the feeling you like me. But—"

"Absolutely right!"

She smiled. "But all I can handle in my life right now is a friendship, not anything more than that. I don't want you to think I'm leading you on, or being coy." She thought of something she felt needed further explanation. "I shouldn't have touched your hair earlier, the way I did. It probably gave everyone the wrong impression. Hairdressers are just used to working with people's hair, and I'd cut yours, so I just didn't think about what I was doing." She realized she'd begun to babble.

"Feel free to mess with my hair anytime for any reason," he told her with a grin.

"Well, I just don't want you to think—"

"Okay, I don't," he assured her.

He pulled something out of his shirt pocket. She was surprised to see it was a single cigarette. As he took out a lighter from his pants pocket, she found herself stating the obvious as she numbly said, "You smoke."

"There's a few of us left in California who still do."

"Why?" she asked.

"Because you're making *me* nervous, and a cigarette calms me. I'm trying to cut down. I only carry a few with me instead of the whole pack." He lit the cigarette and took a puff.

As the smoke wafted around his handsome face and blond hair, he reminded her of Alan Ladd in old movies from the forties, when everyone smoked and it looked so sophisticated. But she couldn't help but feel heavy with sadness.

"What's wrong? Smoke bothers you? I can put it out," he offered.

"My father died of lung cancer. He smoked all his life."

He stared at her a long moment, then slowly nodded his head. Reaching for the ashtray, he extinguished the cigarette.

Sharon felt guilty. "Sorry, I didn't mean to lay a trip on you. It's just that when I see someone I like smoking, I get a little upset."

His eyes seemed to glow with inner lights. "I like that you're concerned about me. I'm touched, actually." He looked away and seemed self-conscious or uneasy, she couldn't tell which. "Doesn't happen to me very often." He turned his gaze to her again and she could see happiness beaming in his eyes. "I'll quit. For you."

She blinked. "Huh?"

"No one else I know—other than my mom—gives a damn whether I smoke or not. But since it makes a difference to you, that gives me just the incentive I've needed to give it up for good."

She felt uncomfortable. "Look, I'm really glad you want to quit, but do it for yourself, not for me. I'm just a friend, remember?"

"Okay. Want to see a movie with me tomorrow night?"

What did it take to get through to him? "I told you before I don't really want to date anyone right now."

"You don't have to look at it as a date. You'd just be seeing a movie—with a friend."

She took a long breath. "Is that how you would look at it?"

He made a half smile. "No. But that's my problem, not yours."

Sharon turned her eyes to the middle of the room, mystified by his logic. It was clear he meant to pursue her, whatever she said. At least he was honest. The trouble was, she'd love to be pursued by him, but not right now.

Carefully she turned her eyes back to him. He was studying her in an admiring way, as if he thought she was the most ravishing female he'd ever seen. His appreciative eyes made it hard for her to think.

"Stan, I need you to understand something—when I bought the salon and made plans to start my own business, I made a solemn vow to myself not to let myself get distracted by *any* man. Not until Wanna Be's is successful and stable. If it were last year, or maybe next year, I'd be very happy to go out with you. But right now, I just don't have the time to get into a relationship."

"But you told me earlier that Wanna Be's *is* successful, and you were hiring another stylist to take care of all your new customers."

He had her there. "That's true. I guess I still have trouble believing it. But I have so much to learn yet about busi-

ness. I have to keep my full attention on every detail. It's like
I have a tiger by the tail, and I'd better not let go or it'll
overpower me."

He leaned forward. "Sharon, you have two tigers by the
tail. I'm the other one."

Her shoulders sank, and yet deep inside a fire of excitement ignited. "How can you say...? You just met me. You
hardly know me."

"True. But, to me, you're dynamite, and I haven't
stopped thinking about you since you fingered my hair and
told me I was five years out-of-date. When you washed my
hair, I nearly—" He stopped short and lowered his gaze.
Then he looked at her again with a sexy fixation in his eyes
so focused on her, she could barely breathe. "I get turned-
on just watching you walk into the room. You smile and I'm
putty. I'll go along for a while and just be friends, if that's
what it takes. I can do that for, say, as long as this class lasts.
But after that, I make no promises. Then this sleeping tiger's
going to wake up, and you'll have to make some deci-
sions."

Sharon stared at him stunned—and feeling so flattered,
so turned-on herself by his wild, bold statement, that she
was tempted to invite him to come home with her on the
spot. No man had ever dealt with her in such an openly seductive way. If she were the old Sharon, she'd never resist
him.

"I didn't mean to leave you speechless," he said.

She made a little smile. "You have. I literally don't know
what to say."

"Don't say anything. I just want you to know where I
stand. I don't like beating around the bush. Men and women
often wind up playing games with each other, and I've
grown to hate that. Maybe it's because I'm no longer in my
twenties, but I'm tired of playing it cool and pretending

disinterest until I'm sure a woman is as attracted to me as am to her. You're honest enough to tell me you aren't look ing for a relationship right now, and I appreciate that. Bu then I need to be honest and tell you that I'm damned at tracted to you, and I'd die to take you home with me to night if I thought you would go."

Sharon was pleasantly shaken to hear her own thoughts coming out of his mouth. She grew breathless at the reali zation that, sexually, they seemed to be on the same wave length—already. This was too much. She had to keep a measure of distance from this man, or she'd succumb to their mutual desire in no time.

"So . . ." he said, studying her face with pleased fascina tion in his eyes. "Maybe we should change the subject."

"Yes, I think we should," she agreed with a grin, trying to breathe slowly and deeply to keep from hyperventilat ing.

"Let's get back to Stoney Ross," he said.

She was taking a long breath and felt her inner bubble burst. "What about him?"

"I still can't figure out why you dislike him so much. He's done all right by you."

Sharon exhaled, wondering why Stan was hung up about her attitude toward the disc jockey. "A bad trait of mine is that I tend to have a stubborn temper," she admitted. "I'm not a redhead for nothing."

"That's okay with me," he told her. "Your hair is divine and I love your energy."

Sharon couldn't help but feel flattered again. "Energy is a nice way to describe someone with a short fuse. But even now that the crisis over my commercial is past, it still both ers me that he apparently feels no responsibility for what comes out of his mouth. It's as if he thinks he's above the rules of acceptable behavior. He makes his living by being obnoxious."

Elbow on the table, Stan leaned his head against his fist. "It's funny. You sounded like that Ione woman for a second, talking about rules of acceptable behavior. This is the nineties, Sharon. There aren't many rules left."

Sharon instantly grew self-conscious and remembered he'd called Ione *priggish.* "No, I didn't mean to sound like Ione."

He shook his head slightly, as if thinking. "*Nobody* sounds like Ione. Whoever is writing those letters must be doing it as a prank. To have the gumption to pull a prank on a DJ, she'd have to have some sense of humor. Yet, by her letters, she doesn't seem to."

What do you mean, no sense of humor? Sharon was thinking. Ione had shown plenty of humor in her letters. Maybe it was waspish humor, but it was there.

"I thought her letters were clever," Sharon said in a just-my-little-opinion manner.

He lifted his head a bit and placed his cheekbone against his fist, as if to think harder. "Sure, she's clever. But she's got an agenda."

"You must be a big fan of Stoney Ross," she said, trying to sound nonchalant to hide her annoyance. "You seem to listen to his show every day."

Stan straightened and put down his arm. "I'm tuned in to his show every morning, yeah." His tone had grown glib, maybe even defensive.

She smiled politely. "Looks like we'll have to agree to disagree about him then, if we're going to stay friends."

She wasn't sure, because of the artificial light in the cafeteria, but she thought he seemed to pale just a bit. It surprised her.

"We can't expect to agree on everything," she said. "He's just a disc jockey. There are more important things than Stoney Ross to agree about."

"Yeah, right," Stan said under his breath as he picked up his cup and took a sip. He put the cup down. "You don't think you'll ever be able to at least tolerate him?"

"Do I have to?"

"It's up to you, of course. But do you always hold a grudge this long? You complained and he modified his style on the air for you, didn't he?"

She began to feel a little guilty, realizing Stan thought her unforgiving. She didn't want him to view her that way. But as soon as that thought crossed her mind, she realized she'd fallen into her old trap of worrying about what a man thought of her. Reminding herself that she'd turned over a new leaf in the running-her-own-life department, she drew a breath and said, "He did change, but he never apologized for insulting me personally on the air. And I have the right to like who I like, and to dislike people who step on my toes. I don't think it's so much holding a grudge as considering what there is to admire about Stoney Ross. He's occasionally amusing, but he's also insensitive, boorish and doesn't care who he insults." She took a second to exhale. "What do *you* like about him?"

Stan seemed taken off guard. He lifted one shoulder. "What everyone but you in Southern California likes—he's spontaneous, inventive, fresh—"

"Yes, I'll agree he's fresh," she said. "Stan, if you meant what you said about being friends, maybe we should avoid talking about Stoney Ross, because I don't think we'll ever agree." She paused. "And maybe it's a good thing we're taking time to get to know each other before... before acting on our impulses. There's more to a real relationship than sexual attraction."

He nodded, but seemed to have grown momentarily morose. He pushed his empty coffee cup away. Then as he glanced at his watch, he looked surprised. "It's nine-thirty! I didn't realize it had gotten so late. We'd better go. I'll walk you to your car."

Feeling confused, she followed him out of the cafeteria. As they walked across campus to the parking lot, she wondered if he'd decided it was late because he'd gotten turned off by their conversation. She didn't know anyone under fifty who thought nine-thirty was all that late, even on a weeknight.

His silence as they walked only convinced her that she'd seriously disappointed him, apparently because she didn't like his favorite disc jockey. She didn't know Stan all that well yet, but she wouldn't have thought he'd be so shallow as to dismiss her on the basis of something like that.

When they reached her car, he stayed while she unlocked her door. She tossed her book on the back seat, then turned to him.

"Thanks for the coffee," she said, putting on a bright smile.

"You're welcome." His eyes glistened softly in the streetlights. "Thanks for the conversation."

"I'm sorry we don't agree on Stoney Ross," she ventured.

"Never mind," he said, his voice low and caressing as he looked at her. "I predict you'll like him eventually. You're too savvy a lady not to recognize his brilliance in the long run."

She had to laugh at such an exaggerated statement. "Is that so?"

He set his book on the roof of her car and moved closer. "That's so. Want to make something of it?" His voice was a tantalizing whisper.

Instinct told her what he was going to do next, and she knew she should stop him. "M-maybe," she said as he slipped his arms around her waist.

"What do you want to make of it?" he gently taunted.

Sharon was too happy that he wasn't disappointed after all, too thrilled to feel his arms around her, to think clearly. But she gave it her best. "I'm too savvy to tell you."

He grinned. "I'll see to it that you don't say anything then."

He bent toward her, but she pushed her hands against his chest to keep his mouth from meeting hers. "We're just friends for now, remember?" she reminded him, making a last-ditch effort to keep her head, keep her promise to herself.

"Friends kiss," he told her. But he didn't move his head any closer to hers, as if waiting for an answer from her.

"Just a . . . little one," she said, longing to feel his mouth on hers, yet fearing what might happen once their lips touched.

His arms swept her firmly against him, and his mouth met hers warmly, taking all she offered and more. Heat ignited inside her and she slid her arms up his chest and around his neck, clinging to him hotly. He responded by tightening his arms around her until her thighs came against his. His hands roved up and down her back while his kiss grew more demanding. She met his challenge with all her strength, feeling delirious at the fireworks bursting between them.

It had been a long time since she'd been in a man's arms, but every fiber of her body told her it was more than abstinence. She had never responded to any man this instantaneously. There was definite, mind-boggling chemistry here, a spontaneous combustion that threatened to overpower her completely.

When she could feel his hardness through her short skirt, she realized this was reeling out of control. She tried to pull away. He held her so tightly, she couldn't. But soon, as if dimly aware that she'd tried to stop, he loosened his grip. It was a long, sensual moment before he let go of her lips, however. When he did, his eyes met hers, shining with arousal, and something else. Something that looked very much like adoration. Sharon had never seen that look in anyone's eyes before. She could barely breathe.

"I'd better go," she said, but only her lips moved. She couldn't find her voice.

"Don't. Stay with me," he urged, leaning closer, his breath on her cheek.

"No," she said, her voice returning. "I'll see you next class." She pulled out of his arms and turned toward her car. Seeing his book on the top, she took it off and handed it to him. "'Night."

He took the book and nodded, acquiescing to her wishes. "Good night, Sharon." His silvery eyes grew troubled. "I haven't scared you away, have I?"

Sharon placed her hands over the top of her open car door as she was about to get into the car. "Takes more than one hot kiss to scare me. But we need to space them apart so we don't burn ourselves out."

He shook his head, his hair bright in the lamplight, his shining eyes knowing. "No chance of that. Gather up your kindling for next time. I'll save you a seat in class."

She got into her car. After she'd started the ignition and waved goodbye, she backed out of her space and drove off. Her hands were shaking with excitement as she grasped the wheel. His kiss had been so heated, she still felt his mouth on hers. She could taste him. She felt as if she'd been set afire, and she was so *happy*. Oh, God, was she falling in love? After one kiss? This was senseless.

So who cared about common sense?

As if her conscience was shaking her, she realized that she needed common sense now more than ever. However much she'd like to feel his hard, masculine body next to hers, this was no time to start a relationship. Kisses would have to do. She would have to drum up all her willpower. And if he really cared, then he'd have to be patient. It would be a true test of whether it was love or chemical combustion bursting to life between them.

It seemed odd that there was such a vital attraction between them, when she still knew little about him. She'd forgotten to ask him more about himself, because he kept bringing up Stoney Ross.

She remembered the comments he'd made about Ione, that Ione was a prig with no sense of humor. Now Sharon began to wonder if it was true. After being awakened, as if from a long sleep, by his kiss, she could see how Ione might sound a little uptight and repressed. Maybe that was why Stoney Ross had needled Ione with sexual innuendos. Maybe, just for the fun of it, she ought to have Ione try a new tack. She could write another letter taking a flirtatious approach and see how the Top Jock responded to that. Call his bluff, so to speak.

Sharon felt so high right now, she decided Ione might as well be awakened, too. Her awakening would have to be well-bred and proper, to stay in character, but she might have just the right ammunition to shut Stoney's mouth.

When Sharon got home, she wrote the letter she'd composed in her head while driving back from class, signed it Ione and went to bed. But as she tried to fall asleep, her mind revolved on Stan and his kiss—and how much she wished she was still in his arms.

6

"Hold on to your steering wheels, Top Jock's cookin' today!" Stoney said at the beginning of the hour, 6:00 a.m. He'd kept his show simmering since he began that morning at 5:00. In fact, it had been days since he'd kissed Sharon Harper, and he hadn't come down to earth yet. Life seemed fine instead of humdrum, for a change. He'd quit smoking and hardly noticed the difference. Tonight he'd see Sharon in class again, and the fire under his hot-air balloon was going full force.

"Got lots of letters," he told his audience. "Two are about Ione, and one is *from* Ione. Yeah, she just can't resist me. I'll read them during the next hour. First, here's Harve with the news."

After the news, weather and traffic reports, Harve hit a button on the board and the latest Billy Joel hit began to play. "Where are you?" Harve asked.

The words distracted Stoney from his thoughts about seeing Sharon tonight. "Here," he told Harve.

"Where's your brain? You're in the middle of a show, remember? You look like you're in dreamland."

Stoney took a sip of lukewarm coffee from his cup. "I know what I'm doing. I just put myself on automatic coast for a few minutes, that's all."

"The last couple of days, you've been going from manic on the air to…not depressive, but…serene. I've never seen you serene before."

"That's me, always evolving."

"But most people who quit smoking get jumpy, and you're calm. Taking a tranquilizer?"

"No need to."

"I know—you have a new woman in your life?"

Stoney smiled to himself. Harve always liked to quiz him. He had the feeling that Harve, who had his own aspirations to climb the radio ladder, wanted to see what made him tick. Harve was more of an intellectual, analytical sort, and he apparently wanted to decipher Stoney's secrets for success. As if natural instinct could be learned.

"Maybe," Stoney answered him.

"Hmm. That probably means you do," Harve said, checking the stopwatch hanging from his neck. "But usually you're bragging about what a hot-looking babe she is. You haven't said anything about this one. Is she ugly?"

Stoney felt slightly irritated. "No."

"Well, what's her name? What's she like?"

"You're my producer, not my analyst. Get back to producing."

Harve smiled and turned back to the board in front of them. Stoney was reluctant to talk about Sharon, especially here, since she was famous at the station for being the sponsor who had complained and called him Numbnuts. And, she'd taken him so much by surprise at this point in his somewhat jaded life, that he wouldn't know what to say about her. Sure, she was beautiful. But there was so much more he couldn't even put into words yet—and for Stoney, who made his living by talking, that was beyond strange. It was as if she'd pushed some button for bliss that he didn't know he had. He wanted to get on his boat and sail off into the sunset with her.

But then he had to remind himself that she still hated Stoney Ross, and she still thought Stanton Perossier was merely the agreeable guy who had walked into her salon. He'd have to tell her sometime. When he'd registered at the college two years ago, he'd used his real name because it was his legal name and because he'd just as soon keep his anonymity in the classes he took. In his private life, he liked to *be* private. So it hadn't been any problem keeping Sharon in the dark about his radio personality and fame. But, to be fair to her, he couldn't keep the secret much longer. Well— maybe for a few more classes, until she really got to know him. Then, perhaps, it would be easier for her to understand. And, who knew? Maybe in the meantime she'd get to like Stoney Ross better. He hoped so. He avoided thinking about what would happen to their sweetly budding romance if she didn't.

The Billy Joel song ended, and Harve gave Stoney the letters he'd kept aside for him. Harve pressed a button and Stoney was on the air.

"I told you I had three letters to 'share' with you, as we sensitive people like to say nowadays. The first is from a woman named Marnie Eisler. She writes, 'Dear Stoney, I enjoy your show, and I'm a professional businesswoman. The letter you read from the lady signing herself Ione gave me mixed feelings. She touched on something that had been bothering me. You do ridicule some of your sponsors beyond what might be considered tolerable. On the other hand, you've probably made Sorrowful Joe's and Wanna Be's household names in Southern California. Someday, when I get brave enough, *I* may advertise on your show. As for Ione, she probably meant well, but she ought to go polish her silver tea service instead of writing letters.' "

Stoney said nothing for a long moment, creating dead airtime, something considered a no-no in the broadcast world. But Stoney knew the sudden silence made people take notice. Besides, he was thinking.

"Gosh, Marnie, thanks for coming down on my side. In fact, I'll frame your letter and show it to my boss, the production director. He's had a few little heart-to-hearts with me on that very issue. To show my appreciation, Marnie, when you do decide to advertise your business on my show, I'll modify my insults to rude jests, just for you.

"And I got another letter about Ione. Ione, whoever she may be, seems to have caught people's interest. This one is from a Mrs. Bess McCauley. 'Dear Mr. Ross, I'm eighty-seven years old this month. I have been listening to your show because I wake up early and can't get back to sleep. But no more. I am through with you. The way you insulted that nice woman, Ione, who sent you such well-written letters, and all you did was make indecent fun of her in such a shameful way! Well, shame on you!'"

Stoney felt the elderly lady's full reprimand as he read the letter aloud. "I feel like I did when I was eight and got caught writing dirty words with chalk on the school playground. Well, Mrs. McCauley, all I can say is I'm not ashamed of anything I said about Ione, though I'm sorry that you were offended. Since you're through with me and no longer listening, I guess my apology—my first this year to anyone—is wasted." He balled up the letter near the microphone, then tossed it to Harve.

"There's another letter here from Ione herself, but you'll have to wait till the next half hour, after the news and weather. Meanwhile, I've got a song from Elton John's new album coming up after this." Stoney hit the button to play a prerecorded commercial and leaned back, taking off his headset. Harve set his stopwatch after noting the number of seconds the commercial lasted, which was listed on the cartridge.

"Ione seems to have struck a chord out there, pro and con," Harve commented.

Stoney nodded. "Weird, isn't it? But I hope she keeps writing. Her letters are fodder for me and good for the show." Though he worried how he would come up with something to answer this third letter. He couldn't let her one-up him.

"Has Al said anything?"

"You mean, the little controversy about my live commercials? No. Unless Al *is* Ione." Stoney almost wished it were true. At least he'd know the limits of the mind he was dealing with.

"But you thought the handwriting—"

Stoney shrugged. "Maybe he dictates them, gets his wife to write them out."

Harve squinted with humor and disbelief. "You really think so?"

"Are you kidding?" Stoney said with a laugh. "Did you read this one?" He held up Ione's letter. "Only a female could come up with stuff like this."

"Yeah, she's got you this time. By the way, I lost my bet with you. When do you want to have lunch at Sorrowful's?" Harve asked as he pressed a button to begin the Elton John song. Stoney watched him meticulously reset his stopwatch for the length of time the song lasted.

"Why not today?" Stoney checked his empty coffee cup. "I need a refill. Be back—"

"I'll get it for you," Harve said, getting up from his swivel chair.

"I can—"

"No," Harve said, grabbing Stoney's empty cup. "I know *I* can be back at the board in two minutes and thirty-nine seconds. You—you're liable to trip on the way or get sidetracked by some passing female.''

"Still haven't forgotten the five and a half minutes, eh?" Stoney said. He referred to an incident a few months ago when he had gone out to the hall to get coffee and on the way back bumped into the new secretary and spilled hot coffee on them both. Between seeing that she was all right— neither had been seriously burned—and mopping himself up, he'd been late returning to the studio, the glass-enclosed cubicle from which they broadcasted. Harve had had to cover for him by playing an unscheduled song and improvising a news bulletin.

Harve left and returned in seconds with the refilled cup. He set it in front of Stoney and said, "It's a little overfilled, so try not to spill it."

Stoney looked up at him, exasperated. "Don't say that to me! You know how I get psyched."

Harve's face fell as he realized his mistake. "Well, drink it up fast."

"And burn my tongue?"

"One of the hazards of our business," Harve said without sympathy.

At home, Sharon sat at her small kitchen table and tried to eat her breakfast cereal while waiting on pins and needles for Stoney to read Ione's letter. She was surprised that he was using it to tantalize his listeners, almost holding it out as a carrot to keep them tuned in. And now other listeners were writing him about her. Sharon had begun to feel a little overwhelmed at the impact her whim was creating. When she invented Ione, she'd never expected all this.

A half hour dragged by and finally Stoney announced he was about to read the letter. She turned up the volume of her radio on the kitchen counter.

" 'My Dear Mr. Stoney,' " he read in his usual mocking voice. "You'll notice there's a change here." He paused to point this out. "She used to address me as 'My Dear Mr. Ross.' A little more intimate this time."

"Your reaction to my last letter took me by surprise. But I admit I'm flattered. For you to think of matters of a romantic nature while reading my businesslike prose makes me imagine myself as an inadvertent femme fatale. But, my dear DJ, I am no such thing. If you imagine that I meant more than I intended in my letter, I can only assume that you must be without a romantic outlet in your life. Erotic notions seem to be foremost in your mind and even color your interpretation of the English language. My word, *aroused,* for example, is a perfectly legitimate way to say motivated or activated. Yet, to you, aroused only means what may happen in the back seat of a car.

"From your reaction I must conclude that you desperately need a lady in your life. Indeed, if my letters are better to you than phone sex, you clearly have a problem. Someone on hand to assuage your physical needs would enable you to free your mind from the realm of Eros to a higher plane. Sorry to say, it may be difficult to find a willing lady. Any female with intelligence would peg you in a moment as a male chauvinist oinker. You may have to settle for one of those ladies who require payment for such an assignment.

"You asked me to write to you again and bare my soul. My dear sir, I have no inclination to bare my soul or any other part of my person to you. As I said, you will have to find another lady. Sincerely, Ione."

As she sat in her bathrobe, Sharon smiled to herself. Hearing her own words reassured her that she'd accomplished what she wanted. She'd gotten back at him and done it with a sense of humor. But she knew he would probably beat her at the game. She tensed as she heard him continue.

"Look, Ione. Who's kidding who here? You may play it coy and try to take the moral high ground, but I can tell you're panting for me. Two, no three, times you refer to me as 'my dear.' And you call yourself a femme fatale. You try to pretend it's me who's hard up for a love life. Sweetheart, it's common knowledge that, even though I'm allergic to marriage, I'm the most sought-after bachelor in Southern California. I get letters every day from women offering me dinner at their place and dessert with a capital *D.* As for being a chauvinist, I'm so hot, women *want* to be chauvinized by me.

"So what about you, Ione? When was the last time you had a night of nights? If you're so high-class and above earthy human drives, how come you keep writing letters to a disc jockey? You want to know why? 'Cause secretly you're harboring a smoldering desire for me. You want me, and you want me bad!"

A boom, as if he'd slapped his hand on a desk, made Sharon jump.

"Oww. Damn! Hold on. Spilled my coffee. Be with you in a sec," Stoney said in an agitated manner, losing his irascible monotone for a moment. In the background someone was laughing so hard it sounded like a squeal. The radio was quiet except for the laughing, and muted thumping sounds, as if people were blotting up the spilled coffee. Papers seemed to be shoved around.

"You see how Ione gets me going?" Stoney asked his audience after about five seconds. "She got me so riled, I rapped on the desk for emphasis and knocked over my cup. Spilled hot coffee on my lap, too. If I have third-degree burns on my most vulnerable area, Ione, it's all your fault!"

Sharon sat at her kitchen table, her shoulders shaking from laughter. Served him right!

"Now, where was I?" he said, resuming his usual manner. "I was saying that Ione's carrying a torch for me. She may claim that she doesn't want to bare her soul or anything else, but that's just camouflage. Obviously she's thought about it, or she couldn't have decided against it. Why don't you think it over again, Ione? Come to a different conclusion. You need to let your hair down, lady. I'm skilled at that sort of thing. I could help you off your lonely pedestal. The realm of Eros ain't so bad, you know. I can...show you all the hot spots."

He interrupted himself with a chuckle. "I'd better stop before the QWIN censor gets after me. Why is it you always get me going, Ione? Maybe you are a femme fatale. Write me another letter, *dear* lady. Let's do this again. And send a photo, too. If I'm going to give you lessons about life, I ought to at least know what you look like."

A rock song blasted into the room and Sharon turned down the radio's volume. What had she started? Why did he still want to carry on with this strange correspondence between them? Her original reason for writing him seemed to have been totally forgotten. She let out a long sigh. She'd have to think about this, about whether to compose another letter.

But even as she told herself to consider the matter, she knew she would write again. Writing to Stoney Ross was a challenge, and she felt as if she'd gotten addicted to that challenge. Doing battle with her favorite antagonist had become fun.

But why? She still hated him. It didn't make any sense.

In an hour she was at Wanna Be's, opening up shop. Tiffany arrived soon after her. After their usual greeting and compliments on each other's outfit, Tiffany asked, "Can I turn on Stoney Ross for a while?"

"Sure," Sharon said, polishing a wall mirror with a cloth.

As Tiffany walked to the radio, she said, "Did you hear the latest Ione letter?" She flicked the switch and rock music came on.

"Yes," Sharon replied, feeling secretive and self-conscious. Tiffany had mentioned the feud between Stoney and Ione before. Sharon had acted as if she barely knew what it was all about.

"Wasn't it funny? I mean, the letter itself and then the stuff he said. And when he spilled his coffee—!" Tiffany laughed. "He's a scream. He just mentioned her again as I was driving here."

"What?" Sharon said, turning from the mirror she was polishing. She hadn't switched on her car radio.

"He made another promise to Ione. He said if she'd send him her picture, he'd send her one of his, autographed."

Sharon grinned as she returned to her polishing. It would almost be worth it to find out what the beast looked like. She knew there was a photo of him on the wall at Sorrowful Joe's, but the restaurant was in Costa Mesa, some distance from the salon in Newport Beach or her home. It wasn't convenient to make a special trip in that direction. "If Ione sends him her photo, she's nuts," Sharon said.

Tiffany gave her a look. "You just say that because you don't like Stoney. If he wanted to see what *I* look like, I'd sure send one. I'd go to one of those glamour photo places and have one taken especially for him."

"Why?" Sharon asked, astonished. "You've secretly been a big fan of his all along, haven't you? So you'd send him your photo hoping he'd ask you for a date?"

"You bet. If he did, I'd be the envy of all my friends—except for you."

"Have you ever seen a photo of him?"

"No. But a friend of mine from high school said she saw him interviewed on local TV once, when QWIN was having a 10K charity run. She said he was really cute. Blond and tall."

"A regular Viking marauder," Sharon said. "It fits."

"Why do you still dislike him?" Tiffany's face had a puzzled expression. "When I come in, you often have the radio on QWIN, for a while anyway."

"I listen until I can't take him anymore and then I change to New Age to get myself back to a mellow frame of mind."

"Why do you put him on at all?" Tiffany asked.

Sharon shrugged nonchalantly. "Just curious, I guess. I'm still trying to figure out what you and everyone else sees in him. I'm trying to follow the advice you once gave me to get on the bandwagon."

Tiffany smiled and was quiet for a while, setting up her station for her first customer. Then she said, "Are you going to your class tonight?"

"Yes."

Tiffany made a big, knowing grin. "So you're going to see Stan. That's why you've got on that sexy outfit."

Sharon had to admit that the short skirt, snug vest and her blouse with a plunging neckline were chosen with Stan in mind. "I definitely want to keep him interested," Sharon admitted.

"Finally going to get off your celibate kick?"

Sharon looked askance. "I hope not. But I guess I must want to, to dress like this. He's such a temptation." She sighed, almost feeling burdened. "He's pursuing me, you know? He makes no bones about really being attracted to me. It's flattering and a little scary."

"So give in," Tiffany said.

"But, Tiff, if I do, he's liable to take over my life. You know how it is. I'll wind up planning my daily routine around him. Men seem to expect that, and unfortunately I'm the type who falls into the trap of actually doing that. Wanna Be's is too important to me."

"But it's nice to have a love life. You know what they say about all work and no play."

Sharon nodded and muttered with a sense of discomfort, "I'll wind up like Ione—writing letters to get my kicks."

"That's right," Tiffany said. "That's probably what her problem is."

Sharon grew annoyed. Tiffany didn't have to be so quick to agree with her, and she didn't like to think that Ione had a "problem." She went straight to the radio and changed the station before the song finished playing and Stoney's voice would come on.

"You're changing it?" Tiffany asked, disappointed.

"Sorry. If I don't hear some pan flutes and soothing harps, I may have a hissy before the day is over."

"You okay?" Tiffany asked with concern.

"Sure. I just need to think about my life, my future and the price of commercials, that's all."

Stoney was walking down the hall toward the classroom, anxious to see Sharon, when all at once she caught up with him.

"Hi," she said with her generous smile, laying a hand on his arm.

"Hi," he replied, then got breathless as he took in her shapely legs and caught a glimpse of cleavage at the front closure of her lacy cream blouse. Her buttoned black vest accentuated her ultrafeminine figure. He hoped that she'd dressed that way just for him, but he was afraid to be presumptuous. She was gorgeous the day he met her, too.

Acting on impulse, he slipped his arm around her, pulled her against him and kissed her on the mouth. Sharon didn't resist. She smiled at him when they broke the kiss and continued walking down the hall.

"Did you eat dinner yet?" he asked.

"No, I was running late. We're so busy at Wanna Be's now. I had a leftover scone."

"Want to go out to a restaurant after class?"

She hesitated. "Okay."

"Just dinner," he reassured her, seeing her doubt. "No big deal."

She grinned. "I'd be happy to."

They sat through the class together, Sharon taking a seat in front of him again. He found it hard to keep his mind on the lecture. His eyes always strayed to the wavy red hair that floated down her back.

Afterward he drove her in his car to a local seafood restaurant. She seemed impressed with his new Porsche.

"You must be doing well to have a car like this," she said, running her hand over the leather seat.

"I do okay."

"Where do you work?"

It was a question he was afraid she might ask. "At a broadcasting station." Fortunately they'd arrived at the restaurant and he was able to easily change the subject. "I've heard this place has good food. Is it okay with you?"

"Sure."

They entered the restaurant. After they were seated and had ordered from the menu, he gazed across the table at her. "You look wonderful tonight," he said, meaning every word from the heart. "Every time I see you, you dazzle me more."

She grinned her adorable grin and looked away, as if a little taken off guard. "Thanks. You look terrific, too," she said, turning her green eyes to him again.

He leaned toward her, his elbows on the table. "Am I about due for another haircut?" he asked with eagerness.

Sharon eyed his hair. "You can go for another week or two. That style grows out nicely."

"Oh," he said with disappointment.

"You can always come in for a wash and blow-dry," she suggested.

"Sounds sexy."

"You're funny," she said, amused.

"You're fantastic. Can we...go on a few dates, maybe? I know you're avoiding relationships, but—"

"I've been thinking about that," she said, growing serious, lowering her eyes. "We...we seem to have something special here, and I don't want to let it pass by because of my commitment to Wanna Be's. You had a good point last time when you said that my salon was doing well. And I am taking this class and starting to learn what I need to know to keep it going. So...sure, I think we can see each other." She grew hesitant again. "But, you know, as far as..."

"We can wait," he said quietly. He gave her a wistful smile. "Not that it's easy for me. I spend fifty-nine minutes out of every hour thinking about what it would be like to..."

She nodded. "I know. I think about you that way, too."

Stoney began to feel light-headed. Sharon really wanted to go to bed with him? This was too good to be true. She didn't even know he was famous. She was attracted to him just for himself, as Stanton Perossier. And it was only the third time they'd seen each other.

Maybe he'd misunderstood.

"You mean, you daydream about...sleeping with me?"

"Yes," she said in a hushed voice. "I can't seem to help it."

"Then why...?"

"Because I need to keep my independence. I'm sort of married to Wanna Be's right now. I can't afford a personal life. If I had a full-fledged relationship with you, then all I'd think about is being with you and it would distract me from Wanna Be's."

"But you just said you think about me all the time anyway."

Sharon began to look perplexed. "I know. I'm getting confused about whether I should make my priorities a priority anymore."

"You've lost me," he said.

She nodded as if acknowledging that she hadn't been clear. "It was about a year ago that I decided to be celibate—"

He stared at her in disbelief. This sexy woman who eagerly responded to his kisses, celibate? "Are you serious?"

She looked back at him steadily. "Yes, I'm very serious. That's how important making my salon a success is to me. I didn't want any man getting in my way."

"I won't get in your way. I want your salon to be a success as much as you do."

She gave him a warm smile. "Thank you. I really appreciate that. But when a man and woman have a relationship, they have to make time for each other. You may be disappointed if I need to spend even the hours when Wanna Be's is closed attending to business matters. I'm only just learning from my C.P.A. how to keep accounting books and so on. I probably wouldn't have the time to spend with you that you'd expect."

"We could live together."

She clapped her hands over her face. When she pulled them down, her eyes were wide as she said, "Are you crazy? Live together? This is only the third time we've seen each other."

A little surprised at his own impetuousness, he said, "I'm thinking ahead. After we've dated awhile, we could live together, assuming things go well between us."

"Look, let's just agree to date for now, and then we'll see what we want to do, okay?"

He took a breath and leaned back in his seat. "Okay."

Their food soon arrived and over dinner they talked about the class they were taking. But as they were having coffee afterward, he couldn't help but bring up her earlier statement that had caught him by surprise. "This celibacy thing," he said. "How did you come to such an extreme decision?"

"I don't know that it's so extreme, nowadays," she replied. "Some people I know are celibate just to keep from possible exposure to disease. And there even are people who wait until they're married, for religious reasons."

"But you aren't . . ."

"No, I'm not a virgin. It was being constantly preoccupied with the opposite sex that kept me from making anything of myself. I graduated from high school with mediocre grades, because I was too busy chasing boys to study much. I went to beauty school and then to work in a salon. It was when I was about twenty-four that I realized I wanted more for myself. I wanted to run my own place. My dad died, and suddenly I was able to do that a lot sooner than I expected because of the money he left me. I knew I really had to get serious about making changes in my life. I started taking yoga lessons to learn to relax. I've always been a tightly wound, short-tempered person. That needed changing, and with relaxation and breathing exercises, I've learned to calm down. I started listening to New Age music, too.''

"New Age?" he said with barely covered contempt. "How can you stand it?"

"Some of it is really quite lovely," she said. "It makes me reflective and serene, whereas rock kept me revved up."

He shrugged and took a sip of coffee.

"And I made the decision to forgo men so I could concentrate on my goals. My strategy seems to have worked. Here I am, a success before I even know how to be one."

"Because of your commercials on Stoney Ross's show," he couldn't resist pointing out.

"Right," she agreed. "Who would have guessed?"

Her flip response was a bit of an affront to him. "You're still reluctant to give him any credit, aren't you?"

"Give *him* credit? I just told you all I went through. I practically made myself over to be a successful businesswoman. And *I* chose his show for my commercial on the basis of Arbitron ratings. I'm supposed to give him credit because he mauled my ads?"

"He made people take notice. You think as many people would have remembered Wanna Be's if he hadn't made fun of it?"

"He made fun of *me,* too," she said pointedly.

"Sharon, you called him Numbnuts. What did you expect?"

She sighed impatiently. "I know that was a mistake. I suppose it was also a mistake to expect him to be civilized."

"Yeah, right," Stoney said with a bite in his tone. "He *is* a Neanderthal."

Sharon studied him, the lights of energy in her eyes fading. "You know, you almost sound like him sometimes. Is he a friend of yours or something? You're always taking his side."

Stoney quickly changed his demeanor, then realized he was covering up. When was he going to tell her the truth? Not now, when she was growing disgusted with both Stoney and Stanton. "Maybe we should change the subject."

"I agree," she said, putting on a smile again.

He looked at his watch and was disappointed to see how late it had gotten. His alarm clock rang at 4:30 a.m., and if he didn't get at least six solid hours of sleep, he was sluggish on the air, he'd learned from experience. "It's nine-thirty. Time flies when you're with someone you like."

"You need to get home already?" she asked.

"I get up early. My job."

"I still haven't gotten straight exactly what it is you do," she said.

He picked up the bill the waitress had left and began to rise from the table. "That would take a while to explain," he said as he walked toward the cashier, leaving Sharon to follow. He turned to her. "Next time, maybe we can talk about that."

"That's fine," she said, though her tone sounded doubtful or disappointed. He supposed she thought he was deliberately evading answering her. Well, he was, wasn't he?

After he paid the bill, he drove her back to the college. When they arrived in the half-empty parking lot, he got out of his car and walked the few steps with her to her car. She unlocked the door and tossed her purse and textbook on the back seat. Then she turned to him.

"I enjoyed dinner," she said. "I'll treat next time."

"I'm looking forward to it," he replied. He studied her tentatively and said in an easy tone, "Is another good-night kiss allowed?"

She gave him an inviting smile. "It's allowed."

His blood racing already, he took her into his arms as she slid her hands up his chest and around his neck. Her mouth met his with such eagerness, it made him delirious with satisfaction. But the satisfaction was only temporary. As he crushed her against him and moved his lips back and forth over hers, he longed for more.

He slid his mouth to the side of her chin and then slowly down her smooth throat. She made a little whimper of pleasure as he hotly kissed her sensitive skin. Glimpses of her cleavage in the front closure of her blouse had tantalized him all evening. He moved lower with his lips and pushed aside her vest and blouse, until the soft mound above her bra was revealed. When he kissed it tenderly, she groaned and dug her fingers into his hair. Her breathing was growing fast and shallow. The pressure of her hands kept him at her breast and she seemed to want more, judging by her wanton sighs.

Fingers trembling with desire, he unfastened the top button, which lay low between her breasts and slid his hand beneath her bra. When he touched her nipple, she gave an excited little cry and he lifted his head to kiss her heatedly on the mouth. Cradling her breast, he teased her nipple with his thumb, feeling it harden to a pert nub.

She kissed him back as if she were a wild creature full of loosed passion and energy. Her fingers dug into the back of his neck and shoulders, as if she didn't ever want to let him go. He readily devoured all she gave him and began to wonder if she'd changed her mind. He'd gladly alter his sleep pattern for tonight if she wanted to make love after all.

He pulled away a bit to catch his breath. His breathing was labored as he looked into her flushed face and eyes that absolutely shone with desire. He'd never encountered a woman who emanated such vibrant passion. ''Come home with me,'' he whispered. ''Let's make love.''

Her eyes ignited with radiant fire for just a moment, but then she slowly closed them and drew away, gently extricating herself from his arms. She buttoned her blouse with tremulous hands.

"This is my fault," she said. "I'm sorry. I send mixed messages by the way I dress and act." She looked at him, tears giving a watery sheen to her eyes. "It's because on the one hand I'm so attracted to you, but on the other hand I mean to keep my promises to myself. I should have met you a year from now. I...I just can't get involved with you right now, both for your sake and for mine."

Her dilemma and her sincerity touched him. He gently took hold of her upper arms. "It's okay. I pushed it when you had already stated your parameters. It's my fault."

She leaned against him and buried her face in his shoulder. He stroked her hair, hoping to comfort her and feeling emotional himself.

"I've never felt this strongly about anyone before," she told him in a troubled voice. "And it's so soon. We hardly know each other."

"We're beginning to know each other," he said. "But maybe we're getting a little ahead of ourselves." He took her by the shoulders and made her look at him. "Don't be upset. We'll work things out. I'm not angry about this. I hope you're not angry with me."

"No," she said as a tear slid down her cheek.

He wiped it away with his thumb. Looking at her sweet, sad, sensual face, he wished he could take her home and hibernate with her for the next fifty years. He had the stunning realization that he'd never be the same after this. Either his life would be bliss from now on because she was in it, or if she parted from him, he'd spend the rest of his days missing her, knowing in his soul that she could never be replaced with another.

He found himself feeling both rattled and besotted. He tried to keep his composure. "You okay to drive home

now?'' he asked, blotting moisture from the corner of her
eye with his fingers.

"I'm okay."

"You want to have dinner tomorrow night, or should we
wait until the next class?"

She bit her lip for a moment while she thought over the
choice. "It might be best if we both . . . cool down a little.
How about next class? It's only a few days away."

"Sounds good," he said, but he knew it would seem like
an eternity.

Sharon felt a little numb as she drove home. She didn't
know what had happened, what had caused her to respond
in such a needing way. Perhaps the answer was obvious—
she'd been celibate for a year. But still, she never would have
thought she could react in quite that wanton a manner. It
was him, it was Stan. Maybe she *was* falling in love with
him.

When she got home, she was still feeling restless and high
from his kiss, yet sadly unfulfilled. Sharon decided she
needed to take her mind off of him.

Stoney Ross reading her letter that morning came to
mind, and she decided to write him again. If she had to keep
herself circumscribed in real life, she might as well let Ione
have some fun. Throwing caution to the wind, she got out
her stationery, wrote Stoney a provocative letter and signed
it Ione.

When she went to bed afterward, however, she couldn't
sleep. Wide-awake, she kept thinking of Stan and how she
would feel right now if she'd made a different decision earlier in the evening. She might have been deliciously fulfilled
and sleepy from exhaustion now, instead of lying in her bed
alone, frustrated and full of longing.

If she couldn't get to sleep, she'd be tired at work all day tomorrow. Was that doing her business any good? she had to ask herself. Being happy and satisfied in her personal life would have a positive effect on her career, she reasoned.

She realized she was looking for excuses to break her solemn vow to herself. Well, she had to free herself of her vow sometime. And Wanna Be's was successful sooner than expected. Why not take advantage of her good fortune?

More important, did she want to risk losing a man who looked for all the world like Mr. Right? So he'd come into her life a year early—she could adjust. Instead of keeping him frustrated with her mixed messages, keeping herself frustrated by trying to hold him at arm's length, she ought to be welcoming him into her life!

She had some more time to think before she saw him again. But she had a strong feeling that, next time, her answer to his burning question would be quite different.

7

As Stoney drove into the college parking lot a few evenings later, he was eager to see Sharon, knowing he could look forward to having dinner with her again after class. He parked and started walking toward the building where business classes were held. All at once, he saw Sharon ahead of him. He quickened his pace to catch up with her.

Her cloud of red curls bounced softly as she walked. She wore a formfitting, sleeveless black leather minidress and high heels. Her legs looked fantastic, as if she'd walked out of a sexy hosiery ad.

When he reached her, he tapped her on the shoulder. She turned and smiled at him. Then she rose on her toes and kissed him there on the sidewalk, while other students walked around them to go into the building. Her soft, eager kiss made his brain swim. He held her close and whispered, "That's a nice hello!" His eyes drifted to her cleavage and the zipper that went down the front of her dress. This was the sexiest he'd seen her yet. "I like your outfit."

"Good," she said, her breath on his cheek as she slipped her arm around his neck. In her other hand, she held her textbook and notebook. "I wore it just for you."

She seemed to be simmering, her body almost vibrating in his embrace. Her eyes were alive with sparkling lights. He wondered what was energizing her. "You have something special in mind?"

"Yes." She leaned up to whisper in his ear. It gave him warm goose bumps. "I changed my mind. You're welcome to come home with me after class."

His heart nearly stopped. This was too good to really be true. "You mean—?"

She smiled and looked at him squarely. "Just one stipulation. It's got to be safe sex."

He smiled with incredulous joy. "Of course. You're sure?"

"Yes." She gazed with longing into his eyes. "I've barely slept since I last saw you. I can't concentrate at Wanna Be's because I can't stop thinking about you. It's no use. I can't resist you anymore."

He held her closer and pressed his nose into her cheek. "That's the best news I've heard in ten years. Why don't we go to my place?" He took her hand, automatically moving toward the parking lot.

"Wait," she said with a laugh, pulling on his hand. "We have to go to class first."

"Oh, yeah. Forgot," he said, chuckling at his eagerness. "I won't be able to concentrate, though. We could skip it just this once."

"No," she replied. "I'll have trouble listening, too. But we have to try."

"It'll be the longest class I'll ever sit through."

She leaned up to whisper in his ear again. "The anticipation will make our first time together that much more sensational."

He kissed her jaw hotly, then her ear. "You don't have to convince me. Just be prepared to race out of here the second class ends."

She kissed him on the mouth as he grew increasingly hot with desire. "I'll be ready," she promised.

He wanted her so much, he could have taken her right there on the grass next to sidewalk where they stood. Instead he pulled himself together, reined in his racing, erotic thoughts, and tried to look composed as he walked with her into the building. When they got to the classroom, she sat in front of him in their usual seats.

The instructor began the class and Stoney opened his notebook, knowing he'd probably be too distracted to get a word written. The instructor passed back the pop quiz he'd given last week and then gave one on the chapter he'd assigned for today's class. Stoney barely had any idea what answers he was writing down. He wondered how Sharon was managing.

As the instructor began his lecture, Stoney's mind wandered. His eyes kept straying to the beautiful head of red hair in front of him. What would she be like tonight? Sweet, tender, and warm? Or a feverish little wildcat in his arms? Either way, it was going to be memorable.

And then, as if someone had zonked him with a two-by-four, he remembered she still didn't know who he was. In one deflating moment, he realized he'd better tell her first that he was the disc jockey she despised. If she found out after they'd made love, she would feel she'd been deceived. She might never forgive him for not being honest about his famous other identity.

He worried how she would react when he told her. Now that she'd gotten to know him, would her obvious desire for him override her dislike of his radio personality? Or was he fooling himself to think she could even tolerate him once she knew who he was? His hands grew cold. He wished he could put off telling her, as he always had before. But he had no choice anymore except to take the risk and hope she would understand.

When the instructor dismissed the class, Stoney felt a clammy chill go through him. He tried to buck himself up, telling himself she was really attracted to Stanton Perossier, so there must be hope that she'd forgive him for also being Stoney Ross. She had to. That was all there was to it.

She turned in her seat and smiled at him, eyes aglow with a sensual light meant for him alone. As other students filed past them out of the room, Stoney leaned forward and stroked her hair. "I'm crazy about you. I want you to know that." His voice sounded rough from anxiety.

"I know," she said in a whispery, purring voice. She touched his cheek and laughed adoringly. "Don't be nervous. I'll be gentle with you."

He studied her beautiful face, a sinking feeling in his abdomen. "I hope so. I ... I need to talk to you first. Let's go outside. There are some benches under the trees."

Her expression changed to one of surprise and then puzzlement, but she followed him. As they walked out of the building, she said, "What do you need to talk to me about?" It was dark now and the campus lights were lit along the sidewalks and in the parking lot.

"There's something you don't know." He motioned toward a wood bench beneath some trees a short distance from the sidewalk. "Something I haven't told you."

"You're married?" Her voice had a suspicious edge now. "You told me you weren't."

"No," he said, taking her hand and pulling her down to sit next to him on the bench. "I'm not married. Never have been. In fact, I'm the most famous bachelor in Orange County."

Her eyes moved back and forth over his face as if trying to read his meaning in the artificial light. "Why would you be the most famous bachelor in the county?"

He took a long breath and slowly exhaled. "Sharon, my real name is Stanton Perossier. But I have another name, a professional name."

"Professional?" She repeated the word as if she had no clue what he meant by it.

"I told you I was in media communications, but it's a little more than that. I'm in the entertainment business."

"You said you worked at a broadcasting station," she said, nodding her head.

"I do. It's a radio station."

She looked at him blankly.

"I'm also known as . . . Stoney Ross."

Sharon stared at him for a long moment, and then laughed feebly. "You're joking, right?"

"No."

"But you can't be Stoney Ross. Why would you be him?" she asked nonsensically. "I don't believe you. You're just making a stupid joke." There was anger in her tone. "And I don't like it."

"It's no joke."

"But . . . but you don't sound like him," she said indignantly, though her eyes were widening as if with shock.

Stoney took on his radio manner and voice. "If you don't like my style, buy time on another station, lady!"

As she began to grow pale, he pulled out a flyer he'd stuck in his back pocket that morning at the station. "QWIN is having a walkathon for AIDS research next month. We had this flyer printed with photos of our disc jockeys taking part." He opened it to show her and pointed to one photo. "There I am. With my new haircut, too. I had a new publicity photo taken because you made me look so good."

She glanced at the photo but did not touch the flyer. He could sense her revulsion. She swallowed hard and glared at him. Her slim frame began to tremble with anger.

"Why did you come to my shop?" she asked. "To pull a prank on me because I'd criticized you?"

"No. I came to apologize."

"Apologize? Give me a break!" she said with disgust.

"My boss insisted I make amends with you."

She faced forward on the bench, no longer even looking at him. "I see. That makes a little more sense."

Stoney leaned toward her, wanting her to hear him out. "So I went to Wanna Be's—with reluctance, I'll admit—to try to talk things over with you about your commercial. But when I saw you, you were so beautiful, it took my breath away. The next thing I knew, you were washing my hair, and I was in seventh heaven. I should have told you who I was, but I didn't want to spoil it all."

Stoney remembered her boastful joke about meeting him in a back alley with her scissors. Seeing her icy profile and her hands clenched tightly on her leather handbag, he wondered if she was longing to make good on that threat.

"And…and then we got to talking," he continued. "You told me about Wanna Be's. You asked me about this class. I got even more interested. I wanted to see you again. But you made it so clear you hated Stoney Ross—and still do— that I've frankly never gotten the nerve to tell you I was him."

He paused, hoping she would respond. But she sat like an ice statue, staring straight ahead.

"Aren't you going to say anything?" he asked.

She turned slowly and glowered at him with sheer rage. "Is this your way of making a fool of me, to get back at me? Insulting me on the air wasn't enough?"

"Sharon, what I said on the air was merely for entertainment. Before I met you, you were just another sponsor. To be honest, I did look upon your complaint as a nuisance. And you had called me Numbnuts, remember? But it was inventive and funny, so I used the whole incident as part of my show. If you had been a regular listener, you would have known to expect that from me."

He looked for her reaction. She merely glared at him with contempt.

"Is anything I'm saying making sense to you?" he asked.

"I don't think you're capable of making sense. You do and say anything you damn well please about people, and then you have the nerve to chalk it up as entertainment." She looked down at her leather outfit. "To think I dressed like this just for you! To think I was ready to sleep with you!" Angry tears flashed in her eyes. "It would have been nothing but a good joke to you—you'd have managed to seduce Sharon Harper, the woman who'd called you names. Ridiculing me in public isn't enough, you want to humiliate me in private, too. After I'd gone to bed with you, were you going to announce *that* on the air, to get a laugh?"

"Sharon, I care about you," he said, reaching out to touch her arm. "Why do you think I'm telling you now, before we—"

She jerked her arm from his grasp and stood up. "Don't you touch me!" she snapped. "I don't ever want to see you or hear you again!" With quick movements she picked up her handbag and books. But the notebook slid off and fell to the ground. Stoney reached to pick it up, but she snatched it before he could touch it. "You stay away from me!" She shot the words back at him as she began to rush off.

He rose to follow her. "Sharon, please. Let's talk it over. Don't just go away mad!"

She turned on him. "Don't you dare follow me!"

"But we were getting along so well," he argued.

"If you don't leave me alone, I'll scream for security!"

"Okay, okay." Realizing the situation had deteriorated beyond control for the moment, he quickly thought ahead. "You won't drop out of the class because of this, will you?"

"I have no intention of ever being in the same room with you again!" She spit the words at him and turned abruptly to hurry off.

He watched her go, knowing it was useless to try to make her see anything clearly when she was so angry. He should have known; she'd told him she had a temper.

Stoney took a long breath and walked the few steps back to the bench to sit down. He felt limp. He'd come so close to forming a relationship with her, and now any possibility for such a relationship seemed remote, if not impossible.

He gazed out toward the parking lot. In the distance he could see her walking beneath the streetlights to her car. As he watched, she got in and then he saw her vehicle back up, brakes screeching, and then speed out of the lot and out of view.

Stoney bowed his head, feeling he'd handled everything wrong and botched his chances with Sharon. What now? Was there any way to win her back? As he looked down at the grass, he noticed a paper lying near the foot of the bench. He bent to pick it up.

It was Sharon's quiz that the instructor had graded and returned. With a heavy sense of sadness, he glanced over her written answers. She'd gotten an *A* on it. It would be a shame if she dropped the class because of him.

He folded the paper in half and realized, with a bit of returning hope, that he now had an excuse to see her—to return the quiz to her. He could use the opportunity to try to convince her to stay in the class. If he could convince her to stay, he'd have a chance to see her over the remaining weeks of the semester. If he was deft, he might be able to break down her defenses, despite all that had happened. He didn't know how, what approach to use, but he had to try. The one thing he was sure of was that he wanted Sharon in his life, fiery temper, sassy scissors, and all.

Early the next morning, Sharon was awakened from a deep sleep by her radio alarm. It had taken her until about 2:00 a.m. to fall asleep, and now, only four hours later, she found herself jarred awake by the sound of Stoney's voice. Angry with herself for not remembering to change the station last night, she reached over to turn off the radio. But just as her finger touched the Off button, she heard him say the word, "Ione." And then she remembered her fourth letter.

Reluctantly she turned the radio back on, wishing she'd never written him the letter so she wouldn't feel obliged to listen to his response. She'd told him she never wanted to see or hear him again, but curiosity outweighed her revulsion. She punched back her pillow and sat up in bed.

"Ione and I have a hot correspondence going, in case there are some new listeners who don't know," Stoney was saying, his voice unusually quick and energetic. He certainly didn't sound depressed because she'd told him off last night.

"She's got the hots for me, but she won't admit it," he went on smugly.

"Oh, shut up and read the letter!" Sharon shouted at her radio.

"She always pretends to be too upper crust for me, but I can read between the lines. 'My Dear Stoney,' she begins. See, she's getting more personal. No 'Mr.' this time.

"I am at a loss as to what to say to you. Your reaction to my last letter leaps the bounds of propriety. I merely point out that you appear to crave female companionship, and you claim that I'm the lonely one. I address you as dear out of polite cordiality, and you assume that I'm panting after you. You ask why I keep writing to you. I assure you, it is not because I harbor any smoldering desire. Perhaps you mistook the hot coffee you spilled on your lap as heat emanating from my letter. How can you imagine I might be attracted when you have so efficiently revealed yourself as an oversexed klutz?

"Believe, please, that I am quite happy with my life. The only reason I write is in the hope of aiding your self-improvement. I would like to see you master the skill of holding a filled coffee cup upright. I would like you to behave as a gentleman toward your sponsors, your listeners and particularly to women. I believe most women would decline the opportunity to be chauvinized—Is that a word?—by you, though your inflated ego prevents you from giving us any choice.

"I will close on one last issue. You asked me to send you a photo of myself. I would like to. But in your perpetual state of slavering heat, I fear you would only drool all over it. Sincerely, Ione."

Sharon sat on her bed, her face in her hands as she heard him read through the letter. She felt so acutely embarrassed, she wished her bed would fall through the floor with her in it. What had ever possessed her? How could she have been so foolish as to start writing letters to a disc jockey? No matter what Stoney Ross might have done to want her to get revenge, she ought to have been above writing him fictitious crank letters!

As he began his commentary, she tilted her head backward until it hit the wood headboard. She shut her eyes in pain.

"Look, Ione, when are you going to get your brain sorted out? You're a lady who's protesting too much. Get honest with yourself! You can deny it till doomsday, but you're hot and bothered and obsessed with me. You quote back to me every evocative word I say. You're turned on by every sexual innuendo I make. You accuse me of drooling—you're probably out there drooling now, just listening to my voice, waiting for me to say something provocative to you."

There was a half moment of silence. Sharon could have died of morbid embarrassment.

"Okay," he said lightly. "I'm not proud. I'll oblige you. Let me throw out a few questions for you to think about. When I spilled the coffee on my lap, did you wish you were here to help me blot it up? You describe me as slavering and in heat. You say I'm oversexed. You really have a lusty imagination! Is that what you secretly crave, Ione? A red-hot male body at your disposal?"

He chuckled wickedly. "Well, look, Ione, there's no reason why we can't work something out. You say you want me to behave like a gentleman, but I bet that's exactly what you *don't* want. I bet beneath your proper facade, you're one smoldering hot tamale just waiting and itching to meet your match. And, Ione, baby, you know that's me. This is the real reason you keep writing me, egging me on, taunting me. You're flirting with me. You're flirting with danger. And you're enjoying every minute of it.

"So, write again, sweetcakes. And send me your photo. I'll try not to drool. Tell me who you are, too. You can't play hide-and-seek with me forever. Why detain your destiny?"

Sharon could have smashed her radio. She settled for whacking the Off button with her clenched fist. How could she *ever* have been attracted to Stoney Ross in class, even if she didn't know who he was? Now that she knew the truth, she could tell that Stanton and Stoney were one and the same. The voice and the sense of humor were similar, just exaggerated for radio to the point of lunacy.

One thing she was certain of—she would never write him another Ione letter. Thank God he didn't know *her* other identity. It was hard to imagine a more ridiculous situation. She hadn't known Stanton was Stoney Ross, and Stoney didn't know she was Ione. Like a movie from the thirties with mistaken identities and crazy confusion, it would all be hilarious if, in reality, it wasn't so revolting.

Sharon showered, dressed and drove to work. When Tiffany arrived, she seemed to sense something was wrong.

"Are you okay?" Tiffany asked as she watched Sharon take scones out of the bakery box and smack them onto the serving tray.

"What do you mean, am I okay?" Sharon snapped.

"Well, you're making those poor scones do bungee jumps."

Chastened, Sharon handled the remaining scones more carefully. "I found out there was more to Stanton Perossier than met the eye. He finally told me the truth about himself, and I'm a little steamed, that's all."

"The truth?" Tiffany said, her unlined forehead puckering. "Oh, he's married?"

"Worse than that."

"What could be worse?"

Sharon dickered with herself over how much to reveal. She decided she might as well tell all—or most. No need to mention Ione. "Stanton turned out to be someone famous. Want to take a guess?"

"Famous!" Tiffany's eyes grew bright with expectation. "Who?"

"Someone you like and I hate."

Tiffany hesitated. "Who do you hate? Except Stoney Ross."

Sharon raised her eyebrows and gave her a sidelong look as she arranged the scones on the tray, fixing those that hadn't survived their bungee drop intact.

Tiffany's mouth dropped open. "Stanton is Stoney? Oh, my God! Oh, my God! That was Stoney Ross? Here in our salon? I talked to him! I actually spoke to him!"

Sharon took a long breath and tried to weather Tiffany's jubilance. "Imagine that. And the sun is still rising and setting as usual."

Tiffany seemed slightly miffed. "You were romanced by Stoney Ross and now you're mad about it? I know women who would kill to have a date with him! In fact, he did one of those bachelor charity auctions last year and some woman bid five thousand dollars to have dinner with him. You got him for free!"

"My cup runneth over."

Tiffany paced around the reception desk, as if cooling down herself. "So he didn't tell you at first that he was Stoney? Where did he come up with Stanton? And why did he come here?"

Sharon repeated Stoney's explanation of why he had come to Wanna Be's. "Stanton is his real name. No, he didn't tell me the truth until last night, when I was ready to..."

Tiffany interpreted what Sharon hadn't spelled out. "Well, at least he confessed before you got into the sack with him. That was nice."

"Oh, yeah, I'm really impressed with his code of ethics."

"Wow, you could have slept with Stoney Ross!" Tiffany said, as if the impact was only now hitting her. "Oh, gosh," she said, dropping into the chair behind the counter, "I could faint."

"You want him?" Sharon said. "You can have him."

"Sharon, he's Stoney Ross! He's brilliant. He's probably rolling in dough. And he's adorable. I remember being envious of you when you were cutting his hair—and I didn't even know he was Stoney then. And he *likes* you. You said he was pursuing you in class."

Sharon steeled herself against the memory of his eyes shining with admiration as they gazed at her. "Shows how hard up he must be, to chase a woman who he knew hated him."

"I think it shows how much he's really attracted to you."

Sharon exhaled. "Look, he's out of my life, so let's not talk about him anymore, okay?"

Tiffany nodded with reluctance. "Sure." Her eyes widened. "What if he comes back here to try to see you?"

Sharon felt weak for a moment. "I don't think even he would have that much nerve. If he does, I'll throw you at him."

"Fine with me," Tiffany said in a willing voice.

Wanna Be's bustled with customers all morning, and Sharon was glad to be busy. At about 11:00 a.m., however, a tall lanky blond man walked into the salon. Sharon saw him out of the corner of her eye as she was cutting a customer's hair. Her heart began to pound, but she pretended not to notice either Stoney or her racing heart. She monitored the situation without turning around, catching glimpses in the salon's large mirrors.

The new receptionist, who sat behind the desk, asked him if he had an appointment. Sharon heard him quietly say something and mention her name. Meanwhile, Tiffany, working at the station next to Sharon's, saw him. She nearly dropped the bottle of permanent solution she was using on her customer's head. Sharon gave Tiffany a meaningful glance. Tiffany took her cue and walked up to the reception desk as the receptionist was about to walk over to Sharon.

"H-hi, Stoney. I love your show," Tiffany said in an unusually high, squeaky voice as the receptionist hesitated in her tracks. "Um . . . Sharon doesn't want to talk to you."

"Tell her," Stoney said in a clear, though not loud, voice, "that I have something to return to her."

Sharon heard this and couldn't imagine what he would have to return. As the receptionist went back to her desk, Tiffany walked up to Sharon. "He says—"

"Tell him I don't want whatever it is."

Tiffany turned back toward Stoney as Sharon tried to go on with the haircut she was giving her customer, a young woman with black hair who was also observing the situation by way of the mirror. "Did Tiffany call him Stoney?" the customer asked. "Stoney Ross?"

"That's him," Sharon said in a dour tone.

She and her customer glanced at the mirror as Tiffany approached Stoney again. "Sharon says—"

"Tell her it's a paper from class," Stoney interrupted the bewildered blonde. "I think she'll need it."

As Tiffany headed back toward Sharon, Sharon's customer murmured with longing, "Look at how he fills out his jeans—great buns! You *know* him?"

Sharon had had enough. When Tiffany came up, her face flustered and perplexed, Sharon said, "Never mind. I'll tell him myself!"

She turned and walked up to Stoney. "How dare you come here again!"

He took a paper out of his pocket. "I just came—"

"Let's talk outside," Sharon interrupted him. "Every one in here is watching us."

Stoney eyed the scissors dangling from her thumb and forefinger. "Would you put those down—"

Sharon glared at him. "I'm in the middle of a cut! This will only take a second." She swept past him out the front door.

Stoney followed. When they were on the sidewalk, she gave him a freezing stare, trying not to notice how his eyes grew more blue and his hair gleamed in the sunlight.

He handed her the paper, which had been folded up. "You dropped this last night after class."

She took it and unfolded it with jerky movements. When she saw it was only her pop quiz from class, she exclaimed, "You used *this* as a reason to see me?" She crushed the paper into a ball with her free hand and tossed it into a nearby garbage can, as she'd often heard him do on the radio to show contempt. "It won't work."

Stoney looked taken aback at her action, staring at the garbage can's swinging lid for a moment. "But you might have needed that to study for the final. You aren't dropping the class, are you?"

"Of course, I'm dropping out. I told you, there's no way I'm going to be in the same room with you."

He shook his head, his eyes troubled. "Sharon, you need the class. You wanted to learn business skills so you could run Wanna Be's successfully."

"There are other colleges. Other classes."

"But this one's the most convenient and its accreditation is good. And you were doing well. Don't leave just because of me."

"What I do is my concern."

"I'm sorry about last night," he said. "I'm sorry I didn't tell you who I was sooner. It was wrong of me."

She looked out at the cars in the parking lot to avoid his eyes. "I'm glad you've seen the light."

"Sharon, we had something great going between us. Don't throw that away, just because my timing wasn't good."

She turned to stare at him coldly. "It would take a lot more than good timing for me to ever like you."

There was a flash of anger in his eyes. "But you *did* like me. You looked happy to see me in class. You responded when we kissed."

She gave a tough laugh. "I've been celibate for a year. I'd have responded if King Kong grabbed me and kissed me."

"Sometimes it was you who did the grabbing," he said pointedly. "I care about you. I even managed to give up smoking, because it seemed to matter to you. I thought *you* cared."

"That was before I knew who you were," she retorted.

"But in the end, what difference does it make if I'm Stoney or Stanton? I'm still the same person, the man you were ready to give up your celibacy for."

"The difference is you didn't tell me the truth."

"I did tell you. Maybe it wasn't as soon as it should have been, but I told you before things went too far between us."

"It still doesn't change the fact that you're Stoney Ross. You insulted me on the air. I could never like the irreverence you're so famous for, anyway."

"I'm sorry I insulted you, but that's my radio personality. In real life, I'm fairly quiet. You've seen how I am in class. Did I ever say or do anything to irritate or embarrass you?"

"Yes. You always defended Stoney Ross."

He eyed her scissors. "I still like *you*, even though you said you'd like to get me in a back alley and use those."

She remembered what she'd said and laughed. "So that's why you wanted me to leave these behind." She held them up. "You come back here again, I may make good on that threat."

His broad shoulders slumped, as if disappointed. Somehow, he made her wish she hadn't said that.

"Okay, I won't come back here. I won't make any effort to try to see you. But don't drop out of class, Sharon. For your own sake, and for Wanna Be's. Stick to your priorities and put your future ahead of anything else, *including* your wish to avoid me. I'll sit on the other side of the room, if you want."

"Sure, and when class is over you'll try to talk to me."

He raised his hand, palm out. "I give you my word that I won't speak to you, unless you speak to me first."

She looked askance. "This is silly—"

"Yes, it *is* silly. But your future isn't. And if we have to play kids' games to make peace and get through a class together, then I guess that's what we'll have to do. Just don't drop out. There's no need."

She eyed him with hesitance. He'd made her feel like an immature teenager. She had prided herself on her growth and maturity over the past year and would never continue to move ahead if she started falling into old habits. She'd trained herself not to let her temper get in her way again.

She wet her lips and covered the scissors with both her hands, holding them against her abdomen. "All right," she said in a polite, brisk tone. "I'll stay in class. But I expect you to keep your word."

His eyes, though sad, held a spark of light. He nodded his agreement and turned to walk away.

She stood for a moment watching him go, wondering if she'd done the best thing for herself or the most foolish. She knew when she went back into her salon, all the excited women inside would wonder how she could possibly have rejected Stoney Ross. And now she found herself questioning if she had really rejected him. Had she chosen to stay in class to insure the continued success of Wanna Be's? Or had she chosen to stay hoping he would find some way to turn her mind around and win her back?

It was strange to both hate and love someone at the same time. She ought to settle for one emotion or the other, because having both was just too confusing.

8

By the time Sharon went to the next class, she'd come down with a cold. Since she rarely got sick, she attributed the cold to the emotional stress Stoney had caused her. She arrived earlier than usual so that she could have her choice of seats. One situated as close to the door as possible would be best, she'd decided. That way, after class she could escape quickly, in case Stoney did not keep his promise and attempted to pursue her.

Early as she was, therefore, she was astonished to see Stoney walking up the sidewalk ahead of her toward the classroom building. Her heart began to pound and she was glad he hadn't seen her.

Unfortunately, when they got inside the building, she sneezed. She was about twenty feet behind him in the hallway. He turned at the sound and saw her. She avoided his eyes, got out a tissue and blew her nose. Both her nose and watery eyes were red, she knew, having observed her deteriorating appearance all day in the mirrors at Wanna Be's. Maybe he'd steer clear of her just to avoid contagion. As she blew her nose, she found herself coughing, too. At least it made for a good effect.

Stoney had stopped in his tracks and was staring at her. She had to walk around him and did so without even a glance at his face. She went into the nearly empty classroom and sat in the first seat of the first row by the door. After she'd set down her books and gotten situated, she realized Stoney hadn't come in after her. Had her sneezing and coughing really scared him away?

Ten minutes went by. Other students took their seats. Sharon was glad when a young woman sat behind her and a man sat across from her in the second row. Now Stoney *couldn't* sit too near her—if he ever came in. Eventually the room was nearly full and the instructor strolled in.

Finally, about a minute before the hour, Stoney came through the door. The sight of him startled her, but she also felt curiously relieved. He was carrying a large cup with a plastic lid. Pausing in front of her, he set it on her desk. Then, without a word, he walked across the front of the room and sat in the last empty seat of the row by the windows.

Astonished, Sharon carefully took off the lid and found it was a container of chicken soup. He'd apparently run to the cafeteria to get it for her. Wasn't that like him? He'd managed to find a way to make an overture without breaking his promise not to speak to her or sit near her. She ought to show him what she thought of his gesture and throw the soup out. But she hadn't had time to eat dinner, other than a scone, and the broth sure looked good. Feeling as if she were compromising her principles, she took a few sips, then a few more. When the instructor started the class, she put the lid back on.

During the class's usual ten-minute break, she stayed in the classroom while Stoney walked past her out the door. As she finished her soup at her desk, she caught sight of him outside through the windows. He was standing near a lamplight, his blond head bowed as he smoked a cigarette.

The next morning, her radio alarm woke her up with a tranquil harp and violin duet. Feeling tired and groggy from her cold, she sat up in bed. She decided she'd never wake up on such soothing music, so she reluctantly turned the station to QWIN. Instead of rock music, she heard Stoney's voice. He was reading a letter.

"'The kids on my school bus want photos of you. Can you send us some? We want to tape them to the wheels of the bus.'" There was a pause, and then Stoney said, "That's the problem with kids today—no respect. Sorry, Kevin. No photos. My face is too classic for tire marks."

There was laughter in the background, but Stoney didn't seem to be amused with himself today. His voice was even more deadpan than usual. "I'm expecting another letter any day from Ione. Stay tuned. For now, we'll have to settle for the news and weather."

Another male voice came on, and Sharon turned down the volume. She wished he hadn't used her Ione letters as a running gag on his show. Now he and his audience were going to be disappointed. She had no intention of writing another one. He would soon forget about Ione, she assured herself.

Sharon wished she could forget about Stoney as easily. She left his show on as she got dressed and ate breakfast, and listened to him on the car radio as she drove to work. At Wanna Be's, however, she tuned in the New Age station. She didn't want anyone there to think she might still have any feelings for him.

At the next class, she arrived early and sat in the same front seat by the door. The idea of easy escape still appealed to her. The young woman who sat behind her last time did so again. She smiled as she walked around Sharon's desk to sit down.

"How's your cold today?"

"Almost gone, thanks," Sharon replied, turning in her seat to face the attractive brunette.

"So... what happened?"

"Happened?" Sharon repeated, not understanding.

"You're here and he sits across the room now. You two used to be the class lovebirds."

Sharon swallowed, not realizing they'd been so noticed. "We were?"

"Sure. You two are the hot topic at break time. Especially last time when you sat here and then he brought you soup. It was a challenge figuring that one out."

"He felt sorry because I was sick, I guess," Sharon improvised, hating that they were the subject of gossip and conjecture here, too. It was bad enough at Wanna Be's.

"Are you still his hairdresser?" the brunette asked. Sharon wondered how the girl knew that, and then felt heat flood her face. She'd forgotten the little scene they'd made the first day of class when she'd fussed with his hair. Resting her arm on the back of her seat, she leaned toward the girl and quietly said, "It's all over now. Please don't talk about us. There's nothing more going on."

"Oh, no?" the brunette said with amusement, looking past her.

Sharon turned and saw Stoney walking across the front of the room toward the windows. But he turned once to glance at her. After he did, she noticed a brown bottle sitting on her desk. She picked it up to look at the label. *Vitamin C.* Swiftly she turned her eyes back to him to give him a sharp look, but he glanced away just as their eyes met.

"Vitamin C," the brunette said behind her. "How sweet! He must really like you."

Sharon closed her eyes in exasperation. Making no reply to the girl's awed comment, she took the bottle and shoved it into her handbag.

At break time, Stoney made no effort to approach Sharon, but spent the time outside smoking. When the class ended, Sharon bolted out the door and did not see him again. She felt a sense of triumph that despite his effort to win back her attention, she'd managed to not only hold her ground, but elude him.

That night, however, she had a dream about him. They were in the classroom. She opened a bottle of vitamins and threw the pills at him, so that they fell over him, onto his hair and shoulders. But the pills were tiny and white, and they greatly resembled rice thrown at a wedding. Then she tossed the empty bottle at him. He caught it in one hand. He lit a cigarette and used the bottle as an ashtray. When he was finished, he walked by and handed the bottle back to her. Without a word, he slipped his arm around her waist and gave her a heated kiss. The kiss was so passionate, she grew delirious with joy. Suddenly he let her go, leaving her dizzy as he walked off and disappeared. After recovering from the kiss, she looked at the bottle in her hand. It was coated and filled with ashes from spent cigarettes. As she saw the gray ashes coming off on her hands, Sharon began to weep.

She awoke very early in the morning with a start, the aura of intense sadness still clinging to her. She knew that dreams reflected the unconscious mind. The realization that her feelings regarding Stoney ran so deep came as a shock. She knew now that ignoring him wasn't going to do the trick. He was in her heart to stay, whether she wanted him there or not.

She was wide-awake when her radio alarm came on. Rock music was playing, but soon Stoney was on the air. To her surprise he did a monologue about the business class he was taking.

"Of course, I'm incognito. Nobody in the class knows who I really am. Wouldn't want the instructor to give me star treatment, or give me an *A* 'cause he's afraid I might blast him on my show. Doesn't make any difference as far as my love life, though. Those coeds are all over me, and they don't even know who I am. Except for one. But I . . . I can't talk about her. She's special. She knows I'm the Top Jock, and she's not impressed. Which, peculiarly enough, is a real turn-on. That's the key to my heart, ladies. Your homemade centerfolds and X-rated letters I can't read on the air are getting to be a bore. Pointedly ignore me—that's the way to get my attention."

Sharon buried her face in her hands with embarrassment, her heart rate accelerating.

"Which reminds me," he went on. "Ione still hasn't written. What's with you, Ione? You were supposed to send me a photo, too. No centerfold stuff." He chuckled. "Not that you would. Just a nice head-and-shoulders shot, so I can see what you look like. I even promised to send you one of me. Which I'd do, if you'd give an address. A proper person like you ought to know you're not supposed to send a letter without a return address. So how about it, Ione? We're losing momentum. My listeners and I are waiting breathlessly for the next installment. Get out that silly flowered stationery, write me something and don't forget the return address! Got it?"

A rock song came on, its assertive beat seeming to underline his demands. Sharon turned the volume down and sighed heavily. She wished he wouldn't keep bringing up Ione. But, worse, why had he referred to their class and to her, Sharon? Was he using the airwaves to try to woo her, along with the chicken soup and vitamins? He'd promised not to talk *to* her, but he hadn't promised not to talk *about* her on the radio.

He must be getting to her. She felt flattered. He'd said she was special. Did he mean that? Or was it just talk to enter-

tain his audience? And he'd said that ignoring him was
turning him on. That was clever, implying that her strategy
was having the opposite effect of what she wanted. As usual,
there was no way she could beat him when he had the airwaves at his disposal.

She might as well start talking to him again. The silence
she'd imposed on them was beginning to be deafening.

At the next class, she sat in the same seat near the door,
but at break she walked up to him outside as he was light-
ing a cigarette.

"How come you're smoking again?" she asked, taking
him by surprise.

He took the cigarette from his mouth. "Are we talking?"

"If you're going to refer to me on the air, I guess we'd
better."

His eyes quickened. "You're listening to my show, too?"

"Only when I get up in the morning. I don't play it at
Wanna Be's."

"Might wake up your customers?" he asked, baiting her.

She pressed her lips together. He was incorrigible. Said
anything he pleased. But the way his eyes quizzed her with
playful lights, she found she couldn't stay mad at him.

"They can't hear the radio when they're under the hair
dryer, anyway," she said.

"That's true," he agreed. He took a puff and she almost
winced.

"I wish you weren't smoking again."

"Do you? Why?" he asked nonchalantly. "You care, or
something?"

Sharon bowed her head. "It's just that it's not good for
you."

"You were good for me, and you're staying away." He stared at her, waiting for her response to his statement.

She chewed on her lip for a second. "Want to have coffee after class?"

"Sure!"

She read the anticipation in his face and voice and wished he wasn't so excited. "It's just coffee, that's all," she said, worried he was making more of her invitation than she meant.

His silvery eyes glimmered as he put on a more circumspect expression. "Right. Just coffee."

Later, after class ended, they walked together to the cafeteria.

"How's your cold?" he asked.

"It's gone," she replied and added politely, "Thanks for the soup."

"You're welcome. You really looked under the weather that night."

"And you took advantage and tried to bribe me with soup into liking you again," she said with some irritation.

"I guess it worked," he observed. "You're speaking to me."

She sighed. "Only because I don't know what else to do. You're trying to manipulate me with soup and vitamins and flattery on the air. It's...not fair."

"All's fair in love and war," he said.

The old adage took her off guard. What was he saying? "Which are we in?" she asked, suddenly feeling a little breathless.

"Beats me." He lifted his shoulders. "Can you figure it out?"

Blast him! she thought. He usually was straightforward with her. Why wasn't he now?

They went into the cafeteria, got coffee and sat down at a table. Neither said anything for a long moment. Sharon felt so confused now, she didn't know what she wanted to say to him anymore.

"So, you like my show any better than you used to?" he asked, breaking their silence.

Sharon tilted her head. "Oh . . . maybe."

"Why is it so hard for you to admit?"

He certainly wasn't cutting her any slack tonight, she thought uneasily. "Okay, your show is good. I mainly don't like it when you start talking about me—like this morning. Or when you sent spitballs over the air at me when we had the problem over my commercial."

"You didn't like what I said about you this morning?"

She took a sip to get more time to think about her answer. "It was flattering. But it was also embarrassing."

"So now you want me to promise never to refer to you on the air again?"

"I know better than to make you stick to a promise. You'd find some way around it."

He smiled at her. "Am I really such a thorn in your side?"

She pressed her lips together, knowing he was fishing. "You just take some getting used to."

"Are you used to me yet?"

"Yes." Her answer startled her. She blinked. "No. I don't know. You keep me in circles."

"Would you have dinner with me Saturday?"

Her mouth parted. "Well—"

"I'll cook. I'm getting to be a pretty good chef—went to a cooking class last semester."

"You did?" This piece of information amazed her. "So, you mean, have dinner at your place?"

"Yes. I'd like you to see my home."

"Why?"

"Because I'd like it," he repeated, as if that were all the reason he needed to give.

She shifted in her seat. "Stoney—"

"I'm not inviting you to try to seduce you, Sharon," he said, his expression growing serious, almost grave. "Would you try to trust me? I think we've reached a point where we need to really get to understand each other. We had an instant physical attraction, and it's probably just as well we didn't act on that. You don't seem to know who I am. I think you think of me as this wild radio guy you can't control, and the image you had of me as plain old Stan seems to be fading. I'm a little of both. I'm somewhere in between. If you'd spend a long evening with me, see my home, let me cook for you, maybe you'll see *me*."

She nodded slowly, impressed by his logic and sincerity. "All right."

"And I want to really understand who you are," he added. "I want to know all your hidden facets."

She tilted her head with a slight sense of amusement. "I imagine you've seen them all already," she said, thinking of the different ways she'd responded to him, from anger to using sex appeal.

"No," he said. "There's still more about you I don't understand. So you'll have dinner at my house?"

She smiled. "Yes, that would be nice."

"When would you like me to pick you up?"

She thought quickly, not entirely having lost suspicion. "You'll be busy cooking. I'll drive myself to your place."

He nodded, as if putting two and two together. "And then you can leave whenever you want, in case I get out of hand."

She didn't hedge, but looked at him squarely. "You said yourself, I still don't really know you."

"Okay. How about seven? I'll give you my address." He reached for his wallet and took out a card to give to her.

She read the Balboa Island address. "Is this a condo?" she asked, thinking how expensive property was in that area.

"A house. It's on the beach."

Sharon almost swayed in her chair. Even a small home on the beach cost a fortune. He gave her directions, since Balboa had one-way streets. After they finished their coffee, they walked back to the parking lot. On the way he asked if she would listen to his show tomorrow. "So I know whether I can say anything about you or not," he explained with a smile.

"You mean, if I say I won't listen, then you'll talk about me? I guess I'd better tune in."

"Good. I have to go home now and prepare for tomorrow's show—read the papers and come up with stuff to talk about. Maybe I'll find some good letters in my mail tomorrow morning. I wish Ione would write."

Sharon felt a streak of cold wash through her. "Why? You get lots of fun letters from kids."

"Sure, they're cute. But Ione gives me some substance to work with. And the audience likes our repartee. Even my boss likes it. Maybe she's on vacation or something. I hope nothing's wrong." Stoney seemed genuinely concerned. He scratched his forehead. "All I can do is keep asking her to write, hoping she will. She's gotten to be a fixture on my show."

Sharon felt a sinking feeling. She didn't like the idea of him waiting for another letter, asking for one every day. She'd go bonkers. As she was still wondering what to do, she realized they'd reached her car.

He stared at her, a flicker of longing in his eyes. She didn't think it would be wise to let him kiss her. Though, to her surprise, she felt fairly comfortable with him at the moment, she didn't want to take their relationship to another level. Platonic suited her just fine for now.

Stoney seemed to read her thoughts, and lowered his gaze. He offered her his hand. "Friends?"

She made a little grin and shook his hand. "Friends."

"Saturday at seven?"

"I'll be there. What should I wear?"

He gazed over her face, over her shirt and blue jeans. Ever since that night he'd told her the truth, she'd deliberately dressed in something demure on the days when she had class. "Wear anything you want," he said in a soft voice. "You look sensational even when you're trying to look plain. It won't matter to me."

Sharon felt flustered and flattered again. She quickly said goodbye and drove home. Feeling more relaxed than she had in days, she soon grew sleepy and went to bed early.

After a beautiful, undisturbed sleep, she awoke to the sound of Stoney's voice. He was talking about a news item concerning a cat that had been found in a cargo container and had unknowingly been transported from Tokyo to L.A. "The cat's in fine health and is being put up for adoption. The only stipulation for ownership is you have to know how to say 'Here, kitty-kitty' in Japanese. Otherwise the cat won't come to you."

Sharon chuckled, snuggling against her pillow.

"But then, cats never come when you call anyway, which reminds me of Ione. I keep calling to her over the air every day, and she still won't come through with a letter. Come on, Ione. Run out of barbs for me already? I thought you wanted to enlighten me, help me rise out of boorishness and turn me into a gentleman. I'm ready for my next lesson. Let's have it already!"

Sharon sat up in bed, rubbed her face and sighed a long, desperate sigh. She had to put a stop to this, even if it meant writing to him one more time. After her morning shower and breakfast, when she was fully awake, she took a few minutes to compose a final, brief letter. She signed it "Ione" and mailed it on her way to work.

Saturday evening, Sharon wore a long, cotton, broom-stick skirt in swirled shades of mauve and teal. Her teal knit top had short sleeves with triangular lace inserts of the same color and a scooped neckline. A matching lace insert sewn in the neckline played peekaboo with her cleavage. She left her hair loose, falling over her forehead from a side part and skimming her shoulders.

When she'd considered what to wear, she'd decided not to dress to look sexy, so she'd chosen the long flowing skirt to cover her legs. The top that went with it was only mod-estly revealing, she'd convinced herself as she took a final look in the mirror before leaving her house. But now, at a stoplight on her way to Stoney's, she adjusted the rearview mirror to recheck her makeup and got a glimpse of her neckline. Maybe it was because she was sitting, or because the mirror was at a high angle, but her top showed more of her than she'd realized it would. She hoped Stoney wouldn't take it as a sign that she was dressing to tantalize him. Re-membering his "all's fair in love and war" comment, she reminded herself that tonight was supposed to be a friendly peace conference at the dinner table, not a victory celebra-tion in his bedroom.

She still wished she could be sure which it was between them, war or love. War she could deal with. Love was something else entirely.

When she found his address on Balboa Island, the two-story house looked plain from the street. Made of wood and stucco with a two-car garage door, it looked similar to all the other homes on the block. She parked and walked to the small side door, then rang the bell.

In moments, Stoney opened it. His eyes shone when he looked at her. "Come on in," he said, glancing at her top as she walked by him into the room. "Have any trouble finding it?"

"No, the directions you gave were good." As her shoes sank into the white nubby wool rugs, her eyes took in the white upholstered couch and armchairs and the colorful modern paintings on the walls. She was impressed with the decor and the comfortable look of the place. "This is beautiful," she said. "And it's so immaculate!"

He chuckled. "Why are you surprised?"

"On the radio you're always losing things and spilling coffee."

"Not *always*," he said, correcting her. "Only once or twice a week. I'm distracted and a little hyper when I'm doing my show, so I lose some coordination." He gazed at her. "I may spill something tonight, though."

"Why?"

"I'm getting distracted and hyper just looking at you. You're absolutely gorgeous in that outfit."

"Oh," she murmured, mesmerized by the sensual glow in his eyes. "I didn't intend to be."

He smiled in a warm, knowing way. "You just can't help it. I told you it doesn't matter what you wear. You turn me on no matter what." He stretched out his arms, reaching for her waist.

Her heart beating unsteadily, she backed away. "I'm just here for dinner, remember?"

"I can't give you a little welcome kiss?"

"Maybe you should get back to the kitchen. Something might be burning."

Stoney nodded. "Something's burning, but it's not in the kitchen."

"Stoney—"

He dropped his arms and backed away from her a step. "All right. Want some wine? I've got a nice chardonnay or a white zinfandel."

"Um, chardonnay, please," she replied, finding her voice a little breathless. Her wild pulse forced her to admit to herself that she enjoyed being admired and pursued by him. Even now that she knew he was Stoney, she was still reacting to him the way she did when she thought he was Stanton. But she'd better get hold of herself. She was here for dinner and that was all. Better not think about what she might like for dessert, because it was clear he had an appetite for anything she might suggest.

He brought her through the room to a table set for two by the window. It was then that she became aware of the spectacular view of the beach through the broad, floor-to-ceiling windows.

"This is magnificent," she said with awe. "You get to see this every day!"

He smiled as he uncorked a bottle he'd taken out of a ceramic ice bucket on a stand beside the table. "I get up too early to see much in the morning when it's still dark. But I'm often home to catch the sunset—if I don't have a class to go to."

As he poured wine into two glasses, she asked, "Why do you take college classes, when you're already rich and famous? What would you do with a business degree?"

He handed her a filled glass. "The entertainment industry is notoriously fickle. I can be the hot young DJ this year and a has-been next year. I may want to get into the management side of radio should my days as a disc jockey be numbered. For that, I need a business education. Even if I never go into business, it's helpful to know something about it in order to conserve my income and make wise investments to take care of me in my old age. Now that I'm thirty, I'm beginning to think of those things.''

Sharon was impressed with his answer. ''I wouldn't have imagined you as conservative. But you're right. I need to think more along those lines, myself.''

''I never used to think ahead,'' he said, walking around her to open the door to the patio outside, where a wrought iron table and chairs were set. ''I only started to a couple of years ago—after I bought this house, actually. Taking on this place was an extravagant move, and I realized I'd better be more careful in the future if I want to hold onto my dream house.''

Taking her elbow, he steadied her as she stepped down to the tiled patio. The fresh breeze off the ocean smelled clean and rustled through her hair and skirt.

''I'd always wanted to live by the ocean,'' he went on, pausing alongside her at the redwood railing, which separated the patio from the beach sand. ''With the salary QWIN gives me, I managed to accomplish that. And after I had the house and job I'd always dreamed of, I felt kind of empty.''

''Why?'' Sharon asked, pushing her hair back from her face as it blew in the wind.

''I'm only now figuring that out,'' he said. ''I've never been quick at self-analysis. But I'm catching on. We can eat out here, if you want, or is it too breezy?''

The change of subject threw her. ''It is a little breezy,'' she said. ''And you've already set the table inside. I'm getting a little windblown,'' she said, trying to keep her hair out of her face.

''You look great windblown,'' he said.

She was amused as she walked ahead of him into the house. "You know, if you keep complimenting me all the time, I'm going to get an inflated ego."

"It'll match mine," Stoney said, closing the door.

Sharon broke into silent laughter at that, her shoulders shaking. She had to steady her wine so it wouldn't spill.

He grinned as he took the wineglass out of her hand and set it on the table. "You always said that Stoney Ross was egotistical. Also boorish. A Neanderthal. And let's not forget Numbnuts."

"Okay, okay," she said, touching her fingers to her nose to hide her amusement. "You should come up with something to call me, so the name-calling isn't so one-sided."

"I have one for you already."

She pulled her hand from her face in surprise. "You do? What?"

"Rumpleteazer."

"How did you...? Wait, that sounds familiar."

"Ever see *Cats?* Rumpleteazer was the playful, skinny little cat who was full of energy." He reached out and stroked back her wildly blown hair. "Just like you."

It was an unusual comparison, but somehow it touched her. And confused her. He tried to rest his hand on her shoulder, but she drew away a bit. "That's sweet, but... I thought you were exacting about women. You said something on the air once about a good pair of headlights, I recall. Skinny women don't tend to come equipped that way."

"Am I going to have everything I said on the air thrown back at me? I'm not really such a chauvinist as I pretend to be on the show. Sometimes I want listeners to laugh *at* me, so I say obnoxious things. Besides," he added, "your headlights look just fine to me."

Sharon grew self-conscious and turned away a bit, not knowing how to react. "I suppose I asked for that."

Stoney nodded, taking hold of her shoulders and making her face him. "Ask for more."

"More?"

"Ask me for anything. I'm here to oblige. I want you to be happy."

She set her hand on her hip in a saucy mode. "Well, I'm starting to get hungry. How about it?"

"You're hungry?" His hands at her shoulders squeezed her softly.

"For food, yes."

"Oh, *food*. I suppose we should have dinner."

"Stoney," she admonished, gently twisting out of his grasp, "obviously it's difficult for you, but try to behave. You remember assuring me that all you wanted was for me to get to know you better over dinner?"

"Right, right." He lifted his hands in a *don't touch* pose. "It was the talk about headlights that got me distracted."

"I didn't realize I had to be so careful what I said to you."

"You have no idea," he agreed. "My synapses make connections so fast, they sometimes get out of control. My quick brain made me famous, but it's also a curse."

She started laughing again. "Will you quit the blarney and put some food on the table?"

He grinned and moved toward the kitchen. "Want to help?"

"Sure," she said, following him.

The kitchen was small, but beautifully equipped with the latest microwave and regular ovens, a stove and a spotless porcelain sink with ultramodern faucets. He took a large salad bowl filled with greens out of the tall refrigerator and some salad dressing. Opening a drawer beneath a counter, he took out a wooden fork and spoon. Handing them to her, he said, "Toss."

"Aye, aye, sir," she said, going to work. She remembered something he'd told her. "How come you took a cooking class?"

"Because I was living on fast food and junk food. I figured I'd better learn to cook if I wanted to be healthy at age forty. I make dinner for myself often, but I still don't bother with a decent breakfast."

As he moved to the oven, he asked, "Do you like to cook?"

"No," she replied. "I'm not much good at it."

"That's okay," he muttered, pulling out a shelf from the oven with hot pads. "I don't mind."

"You don't mind cooking?" She tried to keep the leaf lettuce from going over the edge of the bowl as she tossed.

"No, I won't mind. You work in the afternoon, and I'm off anyway, so it makes sense for me to cook dinner." He seemed preoccupied testing the doneness of a roasted bird, which had a somewhat different shape than a chicken.

Sharon was growing confused by his conversation. "I'm not following your train of thought."

He set the roast pan on some folded towels on the counter. "When we're living together." He glanced at her. "I mean, if we lived together, that's what we'd do."

"Oh," Sharon said, not sure how to respond to that. He'd mentioned something before about them living together, but at this point she was beginning to wonder if she should take anything he said seriously. He *was* Stoney Ross, after all. She decided to treat it as a joke. "You mean if I move in here, you'd do all the cooking? Sounds like a good deal."

"Does it?" He'd stopped to study her, his eyes rounded, quizzing her.

She stopped tossing. "We're just joking, right?"

"That's up to you."

"What's that supposed to mean?" she asked, getting slightly irritated. Why couldn't he just give her a straight answer?

"If you want this topic to be only a joke, then it's just a joke. If you want to move in and let me cook for you, then it's for real."

She swallowed. "So, you mean I'm invited to move in and ... and you'll make all the dinners? What's my end of this bargain? What would I be expected to do?"

He took a long breath and looked uneasy. "I didn't actually mean to bring this up. I was preoccupied with the duck and not keeping track of what I was saying. This is making you uncomfortable, so let's drop it."

"Wait a minute." She tapped the wood spoon against the bowl. "You can't just say something and leave me hanging. What did you mean? And don't give me some evasive answer."

"Okay. I told you many times that I'm nuts about you. More and more I keep thinking that I'd like you to live here with me. Be with me. Share my life. As far as household arrangements, if I do the cooking, then maybe you could do the laundry."

"Stoney," she said, feeling spun-around and dizzy, "I'm not ready to—"

"I know. I didn't mean to bring it up. You asked what I meant when I made that slip, so I told you. Why don't we just forget about it for now?"

"That's a little hard. This is the second time you've mentioned it."

"Well, that shows it's been on my mind a lot," he said matter-of-factly.

"But, we hardly know each other."

"No, that's not true anymore." He gestured with the stainless-steel fork he'd used to prick the duck to see if it was done. "We've had our first fight. We're back on friendly terms. I'd say we've made some progress."

"But, live together?"

"It doesn't have to be this week or even this month. It's just—I'm lonely living here. I'd like you in my life on a closer basis than you are now."

"As lovers," she said, noticing that he wasn't mentioning anything about marriage. But then, everyone knew Stoney Ross was allergic to marriage, so that shouldn't surprise her.

"Yes, as lovers, if we reach that point. I'm not—" he paused and bowed his head "—I'm not trying to push you, even though my desires make me move faster than I intend to sometimes. I just—" he lifted his shoulders in a bewildered manner "—I get near you and I want you. It's been that way ever since I met you. I've never been this batty about a woman before."

Sharon couldn't help but be touched, even if he didn't express himself in the most romantic way. She could tell that talking about his feelings was difficult for him, and she appreciated that he was making an effort to try.

Both were silent for the next minute or so while he transferred the duck to a serving platter and took a scalloped potato casserole out of the oven. When everything was on the table, he lit the long white candles he'd placed there earlier, then slid out a chair for her.

As she sat down, she said, "This is lovely. You've gone to a lot of trouble."

He took a chair opposite her and smiled as he opened a cloth napkin onto his lap. "Just an oversexed klutz trying to make a good impression."

Sharon had begun to take a sip of her wine and nearly choked. She pretended to laugh. "Ione wrote that, didn't she?"

"Yes," he said, carving the duck in half. "I'm still waiting for another letter."

Sharon realized he must not have received the final letter she'd written. Calculating when it would have arrived at the station, she figured it must be there at QWIN waiting for him. He'd find it on Monday morning. "Maybe she's lost interest," Sharon said in a nonchalant tone.

He served her half the duck, cut into two pieces. "I hope not. She's part of my show, now."

Sharon couldn't help but wonder why he seemed to value Ione so much, but was too self-conscious to say any more. She didn't want to take the chance that she might inadvertently reveal herself. As she served herself some of the potato casserole, she decided to change the subject.

"I'd like to know more about the old girlfriend you mentioned when you read my commercial the first time. Did you really dump her because you saw her while she was getting a foil weave?"

Stoney seemed at a loss for a moment as he speared some lettuce with his fork. "My story about the alien with aluminum coming out of her head?" He exhaled thoughtfully. "My relationship with her was coming to an end, anyway. No, I didn't part company with her because I saw her that way at her salon. That all happened when I was still working in Chicago. Your commercial jogged my memory and I used it as a joke."

Sharon nodded, accepting his explanation. "Tiffany still uses your joke with her customers. When she begins a weave, she'll say, 'Now I'll turn you into an alien from another planet for a while.' Most of our customers listen to your show, and they laugh and start to talk about you."

"You must feel kind of left out, not being a fan of mine."

She gave him a look. "I used to. But...that's changing."

He opened his eyes wide and dropped his fork onto the lettuce. "You mean…you're beginning to actually *enjoy* my show?"

She pushed a slice of potato around her plate and made a little upward movement with her chin. "Yeah, I don't know what's wrong with me. Maybe I should see a doctor."

"What about your beloved New Age station?"

"I switch to that after your show's over. It calms me down."

His eyes sharpened. "Listening to me gets you excited?"

She shifted her water glass to one side in a subtle move of defiance. "The rock music gets me wound up," she said, correcting him. "You…you just keep me in circles. One minute you're mild and cute reading a letter from a kid, and the next, you're insulting one of your sponsors or laughing at the latest tabloid gossip about some movie star. You're unpredictable. I can't figure you out."

"I can sympathize. I've been trying for years."

She laughed and picked up her knife and fork to cut a piece of duck.

"You're not easy to predict, either," he said.

She looked up. "I thought I was pretty straightforward."

"What about that temper of yours?"

"Yes, but it's predictable. Someone steps on my toes, I get mad. Someone's nice to me, I'm nice to them."

"Hmm," he murmured. "I'd like to believe that last part."

She hesitated. "Haven't I been pleasant to you tonight?"

"Yes, you have." He looked down at his plate. "But, you know me. I'm still hoping we can get beyond pleasantries to something a little more tangible."

"What do you mean by tangible?"

"Like feeling you in my arms."

She leaned back in her chair. "You're incorrigible."

"You're incomparable."

She picked up her wineglass, thinking as she took a last sip, then set the empty glass on the table. "Has this kind of persistence worked for you in the past?"

He picked up the bottle of wine and poured her some more. "With other women? Never needed persistence. Women are attracted to fame and power. You're the only one who wasn't impressed. You liked me better when I was a nobody named Stanton." He set the bottle back on ice and gave her a steady look. "That's what I need, someone who wants me just for me, not because I'm a hotshot DJ. That's why I'd like to keep you around."

She felt moved, but didn't know what to say, how to answer his appreciation of her. She might be attracted to him—so attracted she couldn't think straight—but she had her own life goals to keep in mind.

He reached across the table and took her hand. The heat of his strong fingers gave her a rush and she didn't even try to pull away. "Want to go to Catalina with me next weekend? I have a cabin cruiser and I go over to Avalon every so often. A friend of mine has a condo there he lets me use."

It was starting already, she thought. He expected her to drop her work schedule and go off to an island with him. "I couldn't. Saturdays are our busiest day at Wanna Be's."

He lowered his eyes. "I didn't think of that," he murmured. He glanced up. "What days do you have off?"

"Sunday and Monday."

"Fine. I can get Monday off. Another DJ can fill in for me, as long as I give them enough notice."

She was amazed that he was willing to change his schedule for her. "But is two days enough time?"

"Sure. It only takes a couple of hours to get there. We can leave early Sunday and come home late in the afternoon on Monday."

"And—the accommodations?"

He stared at her blankly. "You mean, would we sleep together? That's up to you."

She grew annoyed at his it's-up-to-you routine again. "This place where you stay—does it have two beds?"

He took a long breath. "No."

She smiled and looked askance. "Stoney—"

"I'll bring along a sleeping bag and sleep on the floor."

She hated to think of him doing that. "But . . ."

"It's another chance for us to get to know each other. It's just a short trip."

Sharon chewed her lip. "I'll think about it."

He squeezed her hand. "Good. Finished? Want dessert?"

"Maybe later. This was delicious and I'm stuffed."

He gazed out the window at the sunset. "Want to go for a walk on the beach? The breeze usually dies off when the sun goes down."

"Okay."

They went outside and she kicked off her shoes to walk on the sand with him. When they got near the shoreline, they strolled along the shore for a while, occasionally dodging waves. He slipped his arm around her and she didn't object. It felt good having him to lean on when she got off-balance on sand that sank beneath her feet. The salmon colors of the sunset and the sound of the gentle waves had a relaxing effect.

"Sometime I'd like to meditate by the ocean. I've never tried that."

"How do you do that?" he asked.

"I sit in the lotus position, do some breathing exercises and then let my mind focus on relaxing my body. It's very refreshing."

"You can come here anytime and try it," he said. He gave her an extra squeeze. "If you lived here, you could do it every day."

She chuckled and pushed back her hair. "You say that as if it were so simple. How do you know you wouldn't get tired of having me around?"

"Because you add so much to my life. Why would I get tired of that?"

She paused in her stride. "What do I add to it?" she asked, earnestly wanting to know why he was so fixated on her.

He slipped his hands around her waist and drew closer. "Beauty. Excitement. Contentment. Fulfillment."

She wondered how he could say all those things. "Fulfillment? We haven't even done anything to be fulfilled about."

"I feel whole just being around you. I feel complete. Sex would only verify that."

"How do you know?" she asked.

"I just know. I can feel it, sense it when I'm with you."

His certainty amazed her. "So, you're saying we're meant for each other?"

He smiled. "Exactly. I knew it when I met you. The feeling has only gotten stronger since."

He moved his hands slowly up and down her back. Without even thinking, she leaned against him and tilted her face up to his. He inched his mouth toward hers. She made no objection. She wanted to know how she would react, now that she knew she was kissing Stoney Ross, now that he'd made it clear he'd fallen for her at first sight.

His mouth fastened onto hers with sensitive insistence. His lips felt warm in the cooling sea air. A wave of heat went through her and she melted into his chest. Sliding her arms around him, she kissed him back wholeheartedly. Just like each time they'd kissed before, a fire ignited between them. Crushing her to him, his kiss grew heated, his roving hands greedy. They moved below her waist to her buttocks and pressed her forward so that her pelvis met his. She whimpered when she felt his hardness through her thin skirt.

His hand slid upward then, past her waistband, over her rib cage to the side of her breast. He tested its firm curve and slid his hand over it, covering it. Her breathing was growing rough as he found the peak of her nipple through the knit top and pressed it with his thumb.

She pulled away from his mouth and made a little cry of aching pleasure. He looked into her face, his eyes shining from within. His breathing grew ragged, his burning breath on her cheek.

"You think there's any doubt we wouldn't be good together?" He seemed to be making an attempt at humor, though the raging desire in his eyes tugged at her heart.

"No doubt," she whispered. She slid her hand over his on her breast and pressed it. Closing her eyes, she said, "Take me to bed."

He didn't breathe or reply. She opened her eyes and saw the wonder in his face. "You're sure?" he asked.

She smiled. "We've had this conversation before."

"I know. And then I spoiled the moment with my confession. I have no more secrets," he assured her. "Do you?"

"No," she breathed. Fleetingly she thought of Ione. Well, Ione was all but dead, so that didn't matter. She had nothing to do with what was happening between Sharon and Stoney anyway. "Let's go through with it this time. Let's make love." She took his hand from her breast and kissed his palm. "I want you to touch me. I dream about you touching me," she told him with an aching voice.

They walked quickly back to the house. Leading her up the inside staircase, he took her to his bedroom, decorated in oak and deep shades of blue. But instead of moving toward the king-size bed, he went to a bureau of drawers, opening one after another. Finally he brought out a small box. "Here they are," he said with relief. He took out several foil-wrapped condoms and tossed them on the bed.

"Will we need that many?" she asked, impressed.

"I sure hope so." Lights flashed in his silvery eyes as he walked up to her. They stared at each other for a moment, but only a moment. She began unbuttoning his shirt while he pulled her top out of the waistband of her skirt. When she was done with the buttons, he stopped to shrug off the shirt while she pulled the teal top over her head and threw it aside. He gazed over her breasts, barely covered by a lace bra. His eyes seemed to burn with desire. Bringing his hands to her shoulders, he pushed down the bra straps, until the bra slipped off, exposing her.

Sharon stood motionless, not even breathing, anticipating his caress. She felt his trembling fingertips press into her soft flesh, then slide slowly to her nipple.

"Ohh," she murmured. Her skin felt so heightened to every sensation, his smallest touch was ecstasy and made her hungry for more.

"Sharon, you're so beautiful," he whispered, then kissed her mouth. His hands fondled her breasts with adoring care. "You're exquisite," he murmured, sliding his mouth along her throat.

Then his lips pressed into the top of one breast as he pushed her soft flesh upward with his hand, making it plump. Slowly he moved his mouth toward her nipple.

Sharon tensed with anticipation, dying for his kiss on her aroused peak.

"Ohhh... Stoney," she murmured, feeling the heated moistness of his mouth as he suckled her. The erotic sensation sped through her body to her toes. Bringing her hands to the back of his head, she urged him closer.

He moved to her other breast and suckled that nipple, giving her renewed ecstasy. But there was another place she wanted him to touch. She could feel the honey of her body making her moist. Hurriedly she began unbuckling his belt. He drew away and stood up, taking over her work on his buckle. In a mindless rush, intent on only one goal, she reached behind to unfasten her bra, now at her waist. That discarded, she pushed down on the elastic waistband of her skirt, tugging off her panties and half-slip at the same time. She pushed them down her thighs, then stepped out of them, leaving them on the floor.

He'd discarded the remainder of his clothing. They stood looking at each other for a long moment. He was magnificent—broad angular shoulders, leanly muscled arms and legs, narrow hips. But what riveted her attention was his taut arousal. She could have fainted, she wanted him so badly.

She held her arms out to him while stepping backward toward the bed. He groaned deep in his throat, his eyes translucent with intense desire. Instantly he moved toward her and they fell together onto the quilted bedspread. His marvelous manly weight pressing her into the mattress, he savagely kissed her mouth, her throat, then grew ravenous at her breasts. She writhed with joy at his freely expressed lust for her. Using a massaging motion of her fingers, she stroked his back, his firm buttocks, his muscular thighs. Her fingers trembled as she encountered his smooth, thickly swollen member.

He winced in painful pleasure. "Sharon, not too much of that, or—"

"Hurry, then," she told him, grabbing one of the foil packages on the spread. She opened it and gently applied the protective sheath on him. "There," she said, lying back, "we're ready."

He seemed a bit surprised and moved his hand in a long, slow stroke from her breast down her stomach. When his large male fingers touched her slick, sensitive spot, she reacted with a high-pitched gasp and then an aching moan. "Please," she said, pulling him toward her, wrapping her legs around his.

"You don't need much foreplay, do you?" he said, settling himself between her thighs. She tipped her pelvis upward to welcome his flesh to hers, and he slowly slid into her.

She could have swooned from the sensation of his probing masculinity deep within her, tightly filling her. "Celibacy replaces foreplay," she said with an intimate chuckle. "Oh, Stoney, you feel so good. You're worth the wait."

He looked into her eyes with amusement. "We aren't done yet."

"It's already sensational," she breathed, writhing beneath him as he began long, deliciously firm thrusts. "*Ohhh...ohhhh...* This is going to be so fantastic." Tears came into her eyes from the warm, absorbing pleasure he gave her, and the anticipation of what was to come. She drew her legs up over his back. "I needed you, Stoney. I'm so glad this is happening. Do I feel good to you?"

His response was somewhere between a laugh and a groan. He increased the speed of his thrusting. "What a silly question for such a sexy woman to ask," he murmured with amused tenderness. He kissed her mouth hotly. "I'm delirious. I could do this forever. You'll stay the night?"

She gasped in awe as a new level of sensation crept along her limbs and kindled the vortex of heat between her thighs. "I'll do anything. Just don't stop, Stoney. Give me more. *Ohhhh!* You make me wild. You make me need you so." She held onto him more tightly and her writhing grew more agitated. Her breathing had become so labored, she was almost panting.

Stoney's breathing was equally ragged. "Am I too rough? I don't want to hurt you."

She closed her eyes as he bucked against her, and she could feel the length of him at her internal hot spot, bringing her to a frenzied state. "No! I like it," she said, digging her hands into his back. She slid one hand up to his hair, and crushed a handful of it. "Harder," she whispered. Her body raged with need, speeding toward that point of ravishing fulfillment. "Oh, yes! More! Oh, Stoney!"

She writhed feverishly, pushing against him to enhance each forward stroke inside her. Her gasps turned to sobs of need demanding satiation. She could have gone mad with the deep erotic sensation he conjured from her body with such skill, such heated drive.

At last she reached that brief moment of suspended bliss, when she knew it was about to happen. She made a long, thin gasp at the singing sensation inside her. Suddenly she cried out as her pent-up need released itself in glorious, tumbling convulsions. Wave after wave of torrid pleasure swept through her, and she hung on to him as if she were falling through space.

All at once he called her name as his body tensed. She could feel his member throbbing and hot inside her. And then he relaxed, eventually sliding his body off of hers and lying next to her, his head resting on her breasts. She stroked his blond hair, feeling exquisitely limp and sated. She felt a sense of completion and wholeness, the word he'd used earlier. Tears of serene joy came to her eyes. "Stoney, you've made me so happy. I don't know why I resisted."

He lifted his head and, leaning on one arm, he looked at her as she lay on his bed. Tenderly he wiped away the tear sliding from her eye into her hair. "You were wary. I don't blame you. But that's over now." He grinned. "I'm in awe," he said, stroking her hair. "Sexy, sexy Rumpleteazer. You've made *me* happy. My life's all downhill from here. Unless you stay with me."

She laughed at the way he expressed himself. Reaching up, she mussed his bright hair. "I'll stay. Tonight anyway. I'll go to Catalina with you, too."

"Good." His smile showed how pleased he was. He gazed over her naked body. Soon his hand trailed down her hair along her face, stroking her neck, then her shoulder. It came to rest warmly over her breast, swollen and tender from sex. He gently rubbed the firm, soft mound with a back-and-forth motion. "I love your body," he said with reverence. "You're like a work of art, only I can touch you and tease you, and watch you grow aroused. Like now." He studied her face. "You have that look of languor and desire again," he whispered intimately as he continued to fondle her.

He was right, she'd grown restless for more. "You have such a tender way of touching me." She swallowed and shifted closer to him. "But I liked it when you were rough, too, a few minutes ago. I love the way you make love."

She stroked his chest, running her fingers over his nipple. With a sly smile, she watched his eyes glaze with rekindled desire.

"Looks like we're not going to get much sleep," he said appreciatively.

"*Nooo*," she said with a soothing sigh. "Isn't it too bad?" She reached out to pick up another foil package lying nearby on the bed. Placing it between her breasts, she wriggled her shoulders a bit, making her flesh quiver, and whispered, ''Ready when you are.''

She was surprised at herself for being so openly wanton, when earlier in the evening she'd done her best to keep Stoney at arm's length. Now that she'd made love with him, she didn't care. She felt free and fulfilled, another word he'd used. She only wanted this wonderful state he'd put her in to go on and on.

She wasn't disappointed. He kissed the breasts she flaunted at him, then picked up the packet with his teeth and ripped it open. Long, beautiful moments later, they were again writhing in a heated embrace, enjoying each other while the world disappeared.

In the early hours of the morning, as Sharon dozed off to sleep in his arms, she felt she had lived through the happiest night of her life.

9

Stoney walked into the QWIN radio station at four forty-five on Monday morning, feeling tired from inadequate sleep, but happy. He picked up the stack of mail addressed to him, got a cup of coffee and sat down at the small table in Al's empty office to look it over. The nighttime disc jockey, J.J., would be signing off in fifteen minutes, and Stoney needed a few letters to read for the following five hours he'd be on the air.

He'd only begun going through his mail when Harve came in, carrying a bag of doughnuts from a shop he stopped at on his way to work. Harve always got enough for them both. "They were out of chocolate glaze this morning, so I only got powdered sugar ones for you," Harve said, setting the bag on the table.

"Fine," Stoney said, stifling a yawn. He opened up the bag and took out a white powdered doughnut.

Harve took a seat at the table. "You look like you've got a hangover. Good weekend?"

"Great weekend! And I'm not hung over." Stoney knew he'd overindulged, but it wasn't with alcohol.

"Drugs?" Harve asked, concern flitting across his face.

"No way," Stoney said, his mouth full of doughnut. He brushed powdered sugar off his jeans.

"What's left?" Harve asked. A slow grin crossed his face. "You've got that new girlfriend."

Stoney ignored him and picked up the stack of letters.

"She must be really hot to ring you this dry," Harve said, enjoying himself. "You keep up this pace, she'll wither you into an old man before your time."

Sharon may have momentarily used up his stamina, but Stoney had no regrets. Every minute had been bliss. The one worry he had was that her attraction to him was only physical. He wanted more than just their mind-blowing chemical combustion, rare as that was. For once he'd like a relationship that didn't disintegrate in six months or less. For once he'd like to be with someone and not feel that he and she were playing games with each other. He never knew if the game playing was his fault or the woman's. Dating in the nineties was such an obstacle course.

With Sharon, he'd tried hard to respect her parameters, insofar as he could figure them out. Even she had admitted that she sometimes sent mixed messages. Perhaps he was guilty of the same. But other than keeping his identity a secret—which, he admitted, was a biggie—he'd tried to be honest with her.

Despite everything, he felt things were going well with Sharon. No one had ever made such an impact on him. She'd started by blowing his mind, and now she'd snuck away with his heart. He'd never felt so happy and so unsettled.

As he picked through the letters, he came upon one with a familiar flowered envelope. "Ione wrote," he said, startled, glancing at Harve.

Harve, still looking amused about Stoney's love life, watched as Stoney ripped open the envelope. The letter was shorter than usual, only a few sentences. When Stoney had read through it, he handed it to Harve.

I could throttle you, Ione, Stoney thought to himself. The wave of anger passed, and then he felt let down.

Harve appeared perplexed as he handed back the letter after reading it. "Looks like that's the end of Ione."

"Want to bet?" Stoney shot back at him, a remnant of his anger resurfacing.

"No," Harve said. "I've learned better than to bet with you about her. What are you going to do?"

Stoney leaned back in his chair and rubbed his upper lip with his forefinger. After some thought, he said, "Remember that golden oldie from the fifties about destiny?"

Harve shook his head. "Destiny? I don't know. The fifties are a little too golden for me."

"It's before my time, too, but I've heard it. It's sung by a girl, about a guy, and she keeps repeating that he's her destiny. It's probably in our library. Ask J.J. when he gets off the air," Stoney said. The nighttime DJ often played fifties hits.

Harve rolled his eyes. "Sounds like looking for a needle in a haystack."

"You're my producer," Stoney said, using an authoritative tone. "Produce!"

Sharon woke up before her radio alarm went off, which was odd for a Monday morning after a big weekend. She lay in her bed thinking about Stoney and the hours of passion they'd shared. They'd stayed in bed all day Sunday, either talking or making love, taking time out only to eat pizza delivered from a nearby restaurant. She'd never spent a weekend like it. She was both exhausted and exhilarated. After their next class together, she wondered if they'd wind up in bed again. She hoped so, she thought with a sigh, cuddling up to her pillow.

But even as she dreamed of being in his arms, she knew she'd gone against her better judgment. Stoney was going to be a major distraction while she tried to keep Wanna Be's running at full speed. Saturday night, she'd rationalized her desire to make love with him to the point where she'd given in to that desire.

Now what?

She wanted to go on seeing him, but how would she fit him into her life? He'd been sweet about changing his schedule to suit hers for their upcoming Catalina trip. But would he always be so accommodating? Even if he wanted to be, the radio station might object after a while. Carrying on a relationship was difficult when juggling two careers and two sets of goals. Conflicts were likely to arise that would ultimately destroy their relationship. Sharon feared such an eventuality would destroy her. She'd fallen in love with the guy.

It might be a different matter if he wanted to get married, so they could make a permanent commitment to each other and plan their lives and goals together. But Stoney made it clear all the time on the air that he had no intention of ever marrying.

Her heart sank. If he didn't want a wife, then what was her place in his life? He'd said he wanted to live with her, but for how long? Being a live-in girlfriend wasn't exactly a high-status role, anyway. Maybe he wanted her in his house only to enjoy the sexual dynamite they conjured from each other—to have her readily at his disposal whenever he felt like having his fuse lit. A long sigh escaped her lips. Sharon realized she wanted to be much more to him than his current main squeeze, however prized and desired.

She reached over and turned on the radio before it startled her by coming on at its set time. A rock song was playing. She sat up in bed, feeling restive now. By not sticking to her life game plan, she'd allowed herself to get caught in the worst dilemma of her life. But she was too in love to give him up.

As she was brooding over this, Stoney's voice came on as the song ended. "Six a.m. Monday morning. You're listening to Stoney Ross on QWIN. Guess what? Ione finally wrote me another letter. That's the good news. The bad news you'll hear when I read it."

Sharon buried her face in her hands. She'd forgotten all about the last letter. Well, at least now the whole Ione thing would be finished.

"First, though, I got a note from Steven, age ten, from down in old San Juan Capistrano."

Sharon fidgeted, picking at her fingernails. Why couldn't he read hers first?

"Steven says, 'Dear Stoney, I really like your show. When I grow up, I want to be a disc jockey just like you.' Well, thanks, Steven. But there's one problem—you can't do both. Take it from this resonant voice of experience, you'll have to make a choice."

Sharon found his comment strange, but then became distracted when his tone grew baiting.

"And now—I'd do a drumroll, but we lost the sound effects tape—the latest letter from Ione. It's written on the same silly stationery. She writes, 'Dear Stoney, Communicating with you by way of radio and mail has been diverting, but I no longer have time for such nonsense. This is my last letter. As for sending a photo of myself as you requested, I'm afraid that would prove to be highly dangerous for you. You might lose your allergy to marriage. Sincerely, Ione.'"

Sharon winced as she heard him read her words. He'd been right—she *was* revealing her hidden desires in her letters. Thank God he didn't know she'd written them.

"For crying out loud, Ione!" Stoney exclaimed. "Was it something I said? You don't really mean it. This is just another come-on. You can't pretend to ignore this wild, insane passion between us!"

Sharon drew her brows together. What did he mean, *wild, insane passion?* When? Had she missed an episode between him and Ione?

"I asked you last time, Ione, and I'll ask you again—why detain your destiny?" His voice became soft and seductive. "Come on, lover. Don't fight it. Let down your defenses. Send me a photo. Tell me who you are. I won't eat or sleep until I hear from you again." His voice grew melodramatic. "Remember, I, Stoney Ross, am your destiny!"

All at once an old familiar tune came on, a fifties teenage torch song with a young woman crooning about the boy she loved being her destiny.

Sharon felt all at sea, suddenly. To tell the truth, she felt stung. Why would he reply to Ione in such a manner? He'd never used that soft, seductive voice when he was in bed with *her,* Sharon. It was ridiculous, but she almost felt jealous. She supposed it was all to entertain his audience. But still, why would he even pretend to be so intrigued with a frigid highbrow like Ione, when in real life he'd just begun such a sexually hot-wired relationship? Why wasn't he mentioning his new girlfriend on the air again instead? What was the big deal about Ione, anyway? Sharon never had understood why he'd paid so much attention to her letters in the first place.

Well, if he was obsessed with Ione, it was just too bad for him! Stoney could beg Ione all he wanted; he was never going to hear from that prissy hussy again!

Early Monday morning on Catalina Island, Stoney woke up with a start, thinking he was late for work. But after glancing around the time-share condo bedroom, he realized where he was and that he had the day off. He looked at the pillow next to him, thinking he'd see Sharon, but the other half of the bed was empty. He sat up and looked around, wondering what had happened to her. The door to the bathroom was open and the room unlit. He got up and walked into the living room and noticed the sliding glass door to the front patio was open.

There he found Sharon, still wearing her lavender silk nightshirt, sitting crossed-legged on a towel—the lotus position, he guessed—her eyes closed, a hand on each knee, inhaling deeply, then exhaling very slowly. Her mane of red hair floated down her back in the light breeze, a glorious color in the morning sunshine. She sat facing toward the blue sky and sea, and the picturesque harbor town of Avalon. How calm, how mysteriously serene she looked. How different she appeared to him now than when she was in his arms last night, making love. Then she was a teasing tigress. Now she was more like a beautiful sphinx.

What an enigma he'd discovered in her. Would he ever be able to understand her, even guess at how her mind worked, intuit her private thoughts? She kept him guessing constantly, sometimes so much so that it was hard for him to disguise his confusion. What did she think of him? Had she really forgiven him for being Stoney Ross? She might be wild for him in bed, but how did she feel about him when she was busy working at Wanna Be's, or when she was home

alone? Did the doubts and disdain she once held for him
sometimes creep back into her mind?

He exhaled slowly, much as he saw Sharon doing. These
were questions he couldn't answer yet. But he intended to
learn all he could about her unpredictable psyche, one way
or another.

After a simple breakfast of toast, eggs and orange juice,
which they'd bought after they arrived in Avalon, Sharon
was in the condo's small kitchen with Stoney, doing their
few dishes. Sharon liked the place, which was within walking distance of the beach and also had a nice view of the
ocean and the crescent-shaped harbor. She was already
dressed in her bikini, wearing a long blouse as a cover-up,
because they'd planned to go to the beach after breakfast.

They'd arrived around noon yesterday on Stoney's boat,
the *Dee Jay*. In the afternoon they'd gone for a swim and
relaxed. In the evening, after dinner at an Italian restaurant, they'd come back to the condo and made love. So far,
their weekend had been idyllic. She'd refrained from mentioning Ione, though it was on her mind. She didn't want to
risk spoiling their minivacation together.

Thinking of the name of his boat, she remembered a
question she'd meant to ask before. "How did you decide
to be a disc jockey?" She handed him a cup she'd dried with
a towel.

He looked thoughtful as he put the cup into the cabinet
near the sink. "I was in college in Ohio taking Liberal Arts
and Sciences, without a clue what I wanted to do with my
life. The college had a radio station, and on a bulletin
board, I saw an advertisement for a job there. They needed
someone to keep their library in order and go on the air once
in a while, if necessary."

"Library?"

"Most everything is on cartridge tapes nowadays and filed away. Even the prerecorded commercials. Though most stations have old phonograph records in their libraries, too."

"Oh, I see," Sharon said, picking up another cup to dry.

"I got interested working there and switched my major to TV and Radio Broadcasting. After only minimum training, I had to take over for a DJ who had a high fever and collapsed while on the air. I was a natural. I was scared for about one minute, knowing my voice was going out to the whole campus, and then I was hooked. They gave me a permanent spot. Pretty soon I was getting fan letters from coeds. And soon after that, a station in Dayton offered me a real job. I quit college and took it. I figured I knew instinctively how to do this, so what did I need a college degree for? I was so obsessed with radio, I couldn't concentrate on my classes anyway. And it hasn't changed. I've never been so hooked on anything." He turned his silver blue eyes on her. "Until I met you."

Sharon smiled at the compliment, but was wary of taking him too seriously. Suddenly words slipped out of her mouth. "I thought it was Ione you were hooked on."

He blinked. "Ione? Why do you say that?"

"Because you said it on the air—you have a mad, wild passion for her."

He nodded. "So?"

Sharon couldn't help but be a little ticked. "So? So how can you say you're hooked on me, when you have this *mad passion* for Ione?"

He grinned and leaned against the counter. "You sound jealous."

Sharon gritted her teeth, hating to acknowledge that she was. "It's not jealousy," she said. "It's just irritating to hear you make such a fuss on the air over someone you've never even met—a frigid prig, to boot!''

He laughed, as if enjoying her choice of words. "A *frigid prig,* Sharon? That's unkind. Ione has a wry, stylish sense of humor.''

"Then why do you tease her and make fun of her?''

"Because I want more of her humor. It's good for the show, and I love it. I wish I knew who she was.''

"*Love* it?'' Sharon didn't know what to think. "Why? What's so special about some nutty person out there who spends time thinking up letters that do nothing but put you down?'' She was far too embarrassed to ever tell him *she* was the nutty person.

His eyes twinkled. "Ione's a tease. I like women who tease.''

"I guess so!'' Sharon shot back, knowing how much he liked it when *she* teased him. But she hadn't expected him to enjoy teasing from other women, as well.

She had to keep reminding herself that the other woman in this case was her. But Stoney didn't know that.

He studied her in silence for a long moment, his expression growing more grim, more and more disappointed. "Don't you think you're making way too much of it?''

She tried to read him. What was he saying? If Ione actually had been another woman, Sharon felt she would have a right to be jealous that Stoney spent time thinking about someone else. Perhaps he was disappointed because he felt Sharon was unsophisticated, expecting him not to be attracted to others while he and she were lovers. Stoney was famous, after all, and used to having lots of females chasing him. Perhaps his feelings for Sharon weren't so profound as hers were for him. Perhaps he simply was not capable of caring for only one woman.

"So many women," she murmured. "So little time."

"What?"

She tried to smile and make light of it. "Maybe that's your motto."

"Sharon—"

Instinctively she interrupted him and changed the subject, not wanting to endure any more discussion about Ione. "You're about due for a haircut. Should I give you one before we go to the beach?"

He seemed taken off guard. "A haircut?"

"I brought my scissors along because I'd noticed you needed a trim. Should I cut it outside on the patio? That way we won't have to sweep the floor."

"Sure," he said with a confused smile.

In a few minutes, Stoney was sitting in a deck chair on the patio, and Sharon was combing and snipping. She'd taken off her cover-up because the sleeves got in her way, and it was getting warm anyway. She'd wet his hair for the cut, but it was drying quickly in the sun.

As she worked, she relaxed, doing something she enjoyed. She asked him about Catalina and his boat, keeping the topic as far away from radio and Ione as possible. She didn't want to make another slip and say something she shouldn't.

When she'd almost finished the cut, she moved around to the front of him, combed through his hair and made a few touch-up snips. She glanced at his face and found him dreamy eyed. It was only then she realized that as she bent over him in her bikini, he was getting an eyeful.

When she paused and chuckled at his fixated expression, he looked up at her mischievously and pulled her onto his lap.

"How can I get my hair to grow faster, so you can do this more often?" he asked.

"There are certain vitamins—" she began, but was interrupted by a sound kiss on the mouth. She experienced a melting feeling again, and it had nothing to do with the bright sun. When the heated kiss ended, she said, "You seem pretty healthy to me." She tossed her scissors and comb onto the small round table next to the chair, then ran her fingers through his hair. He closed his eyes in pleasure.

She kissed him on the mouth, then brought his head down to her cleavage. His hot, moist kisses on the inner curves of her breasts made her gasp with delight. All at once she felt him tug the knot at the back of her neck, which held her bikini top in place. The two spaghetti straps fell down her arms, revealing more of her breasts. His kisses became more ardent, and soon he was biting and suckling her nipple.

Suddenly she realized they were outside and visible to passersby. "Stoney, let's go inside," she whispered.

"Back to bed," he said with a little kiss on her chin. He stood, lifting her in his arms at the same time. He carried her back to their unmade bed and set her down on the sheets, then lay down beside her.

In moments both were undressed, embracing each other with their own brand of wild, tender passion. He knew exactly how to bring her to one exquisite climax after another, until she was satiated and limp in his arms.

As she recovered, taking deep, quick breaths, her cheek against his shoulder, damp from perspiration, she knew she could never let him go, whether he flirted with other women or not. Maybe she was losing some of her pride, but she needed him. She felt so fulfilled with him. She loved him.

As if echoing her thoughts, he said, "We're so compatible, like we were made for each other. Being in bed with you is so...comfortable and natural."

"I know," she said, drawing away to look at his face. His warm eyes showed his sublime contentment. "It's like we've been married for years." As soon as she said the words, she regretted it, realizing it was another slip. Even though she wondered whether she would ever be married to him, she didn't want him to think she was hinting for it. If he married her, she wanted it to be his idea.

Stoney didn't recoil, as she half expected. Instead he laughed, his eyes sparkling. He snuggled against her, his cheek on her hair. She couldn't see his face anymore, but she heard him say, in a jaunty way, "If Stoney Ross got married, it would be a major public event."

Sharon made no reply, feeling a little stunned and confused by his quip. Then she realized what he must have meant: He believed the possibility of him exchanging wedding vows with anyone was so unlikely, it would certainly make headlines if it happened. Especially since he'd always claimed on the air to be allergic to marriage. How could she forget? How could she be so foolish as to even entertain the hope?

A tear slid from her eye as she lay back on the pillow. Stoney was blissfully dozing on her shoulder, unaware of the distress he'd given her with his amused, blithe statement of fact. She knew now she would probably wind up with a broken heart for falling in love with him.

Perhaps she should leave him now, before her love grew beyond the point of recovery. If she got too used to him in her life, how could she ever adjust to losing him when he grew tired of her or met someone else?

Oh, she'd somehow manage to reconstruct her life again, she supposed. She still would have Wanna Be's. But she wanted Stoney, too. Waiting and wondering when their relationship would end would be agony. She should be smart and be the one to break it off.

One day she would, she promised herself. But...not today.

She smoothed his blond hair with her hand and bent her head, so that her cheek rested against his hair. Perfection only came once or twice in a lifetime. She might as well enjoy it while she had it.

10

Sharon tried to go about her life as usual over the following week, which had begun with such bittersweet bliss in Avalon. But the week wasn't normal at all. At Wanna Be's, Tiffany and the others all fished for tidbits from her about her island retreat with their favorite DJ. Dodging their queries took emotional energy, and she felt drained by the week's end.

Something else disturbed her equilibrium, too. Every single morning on the air, Stoney made a plea to Ione, sometimes two and three times during each show, begging her to write to him again. Sharon's fears about his philandering ways intensified. But as the week wore on, she began to grow angry. What was the matter with him, to go on and on about Ione this way? Maybe he thought of it as entertainment for his show, but it was beginning to get tiresome.

Seeing him in class and on the weekend following their Catalina trip was difficult. She felt stiff around him and studiously refrained from mentioning Ione. He continued to seem disappointed in some way—with her, she feared. They didn't even make love. She realized his fixation with Ione was beginning to ruin their relationship. Why had she ever written those damn letters?

She had Monday off, and was glad to be able to stay home by herself. After sleeping a little late, she turned on her radio while eating breakfast at her kitchen table. Stoney was reading a letter from a man.

"'Hey, Top Jock! I wish I had your problems. Your life must be real rough. All those fan letters and provocative photos you say women send you, and you're hung up on some babe who does nothing but dis you? You used to be a cool DJ and a cool dude. Lately, you sound like a lovesick calf, always mooing to Ione to write again. Forget Ione, man! For all you know, she may look like a brontosaurus. So she dumped you. It happens to every guy sooner or later. Get over it! Say good riddance. There are other women on the planet. Yours truly, T. Sharkey.'"

After reading the letter, Stoney added, "In parenthesis under his signature, he explains that the T stands for Tomcat." He chuckled. "Okay, Tom, thanks for the advice. Sorry I can't take it. There *is* no other woman on the planet for me. Ione's prediction was right—she's made me lose my allergy to marriage. So, here's a bulletin for you, Ione—I love you! If you come down here to the QWIN station and identify yourself, I'll marry you. That's right, I'm talking about a wedding with a minister, flowers, vows, the whole bit."

Sharon's spoon clattered into her cereal bowl as she listened, dumbfounded. Love? He'd never said that word to *her.* And marriage? A wedding? It must be a publicity stunt. Her heart pounding, she turned up the volume as he continued.

"I'll stay here all day at the station and wait for you, Ione. Don't disappoint me. Be brave. Face the music. We're destined for each other, you *know* that!"

The old song from the fifties suddenly came on, the one he'd played before with lyrics about destiny. Sharon pushed her hair off her face, her hands above her ears. This was incredible! Maybe his ratings were falling and he needed something to juice them up. He wouldn't actually marry somebody he'd never met.

Sharon set her elbow on the table, the heel of her hand at her forehead. Unless somehow he knew she was Ione. But how would he know? She'd never told anyone, not a single soul. There was no way he could guess, either. She'd used high-flown language in the Ione letters, a manner of speaking she never used in real life. Oh, it had to be a publicity stunt.

But if he was actually expecting someone named Ione to appear at the QWIN station, was the "wedding" to be a fake one on the air? Had he hired some actress to pretend to be Ione, so he could "marry" her as he'd promised his audience? A mock wedding would certainly increase his ratings. Sharon couldn't believe his irreverence toward the institution of marriage. She ought to show up, just to see what he'd do!

Her humor failed to amuse her. Sharon shook her head in deepening dismay. Of all the men on the globe, why had she fallen in love with Stoney Ross?

Sharon's notion that it was all a publicity stunt seemed to be substantiated by the TV News at 4:00 p.m. One news report featured live coverage of a line of women waiting outside the QWIN radio station, all claiming to be Ione. The male reporter interviewed two of them. One was a brunette who said her given name actually *was* Ione and showed the reporter her driver's license as proof. She said breathlessly, "I've had a crazy crush on Stoney for a year, and now I understand why. Destiny drew me to him—because I was fated to marry him."

Sharon rolled her eyes. Next the reporter talked to the woman behind her, a pleasant-looking woman of about fifty in a lavender sweatshirt with the face of a white long-haired cat painted on the front. Giggling, she admitted, "No, I'm not really Ione. I just came here hoping to meet him in person. He's my favorite DJ."

The reporter turned back toward the camera and with amusement warned, "Each woman's handwriting will be tested to see if it matches the letters sent to Stoney. Those letters, I'm told by a representative from the station, are under lock and key. So far, no one's handwriting has matched."

Handwriting. Sharon felt a moment of panic. How absurd that she'd never thought of the obvious. But as her mind raced, she couldn't remember any occasion on which Stoney had watched her write anything, much less have a sample to compare the letters with. She was safe, she thought, exhaling.

Then her breath caught in her throat. The quiz. The pop quiz she'd dropped, that he'd brought back to her the next day. She'd thrown it into the garbage immediately, but he'd had it overnight—long enough to recognize it, even photocopy it, and compare it with Ione's handwriting.

Her hands grew icy. Stoney knew!

Sharon felt mortified. He'd probably known she was Ione when he brought the quiz back to her. Maybe he'd even meant it as a signal to her that he knew. Maybe he'd wanted her to admit it. But being angry with him at the time, she'd been oblivious to his hint.

He's been on to me all this time, she thought with humiliation. He knew when they made love the first time. He knew when they went to Catalina. Why didn't he just *say* he'd figured it out? Why was he turning the whole thing into such a circus?

She thought back to their first skirmishes over her commercial and how he'd responded to her with gibes on the air. When he found her quiz and recognized her handwriting, he probably knew then that she'd retaliated by writing him the Ione letters. But he kept his knowledge a secret so he could invent this ''wedding'' to get back at her, because she'd managed to trick him. He'd even said it in Avalon: *If Stoney Ross got married, it would be a major public event.* So it was becoming—an event designed solely to embarrass her. And how he was getting the publicity he wanted! Lines of women. TV reporters. Live interviews—

Sharon gasped suddenly and clapped her hand over her mouth. On TV there was a commotion amongst the line of women—they'd started screaming. The beaming young reporter said, ''We've been hoping Stoney would come out to speak with us, and here he is!''

The camera shifted to take in the tall, blond man standing next to the reporter. Stoney was smiling, his beautiful hair shifting in the breeze.

''Are you serious about marrying Ione?'' the reporter asked. He turned his microphone to Stoney.

''You bet!''

''But you don't know what she looks like,'' the reporter said.

Stoney shrugged nonchalantly. ''She's got beautiful handwriting, so she must be gorgeous.''

''That's logical,'' the reporter quipped. ''What do you think about this line of women, all claiming they're Ione?''

"Impostors," Stoney replied. "There's only one Ione. And if she doesn't get her little rear end down here pretty soon, I may have to stay a bachelor."

"You heard it here first." The reporter signed off with a grin. The anchorman came on again with another news item. Sharon turned down her TV with a shaky hand so she could think. She didn't know whether to believe Stoney or not. There was a seeming honesty in his voice. Did he really mean he'd marry her? But if he wanted to marry her, why hadn't he said so on Catalina? Why go through all this hokum?

What would happen if she went down to the station? Would he publicly embarrass her? Or...would he throw his arms around her and ask her to set a date for a real wedding?

Sharon didn't have nerve enough to find out. As she listened to the local TV newscasts that evening, most of which covered the event, she grew more and more mortified at being the unseen focal point of the hubbub. QWIN ought to give her a commission for bringing them, and Stoney, so much publicity, she thought with rancor. Finally she turned the TV off and went to bed.

But she lay awake most of the night, her thoughts revolving between the two possibilities—*Is he serious? Or is he intent on humiliating me?*

By morning she realized it was no use. She was embarrassed and humiliated already. If she went down to the station, at least she'd be ending all the hullabaloo over Ione. He'd told Ione to "face the music." Sharon realized she had no other choice.

She got out of bed about 4:00 a.m. and showered. Perhaps out of some subliminal need to appear tough, she threw on black jeans, a white shirt and boots.

As she drove to the QWIN station, she turned on her car radio and listened to Stoney, who came on the air at five. He sounded more crabby than irreverent this morning. "Look, ladies, if you aren't Ione, you're going to get found out, so why don't you just do yourself and us a favor and stay home? After the lineup of females outside our door got covered on TV yesterday afternoon, more and more women showed up, and by evening we had to call in security to keep order. As for *you,* Ione—the *real* Ione—I'm getting ticked!"

"Tough!" she yelled at her radio.

"If you don't show up by the end of my show today, I'll...I'll...well, I don't know what the hell I'll do. By the time I go off the air, I'll think of something, though! Let's have some *thinking* music!"

An old song by Billy Joel came on, the one about wandering in his sleep. Sharon turned the volume down and tried to concentrate on driving. She'd almost made a wrong turn.

At last she arrived at the QWIN station, an unimposing one-story building on a corner. The parking lot had only a few cars and there was no line of women. Too early, she supposed. At least she wouldn't have to face any reporters, as she'd feared she would.

Sweating a bit, her palms clammy, Sharon got out of her car and made herself walk to the door. When she entered, she found herself in a small reception area. At first the room was empty, but then a man walked in. She'd somehow expected to see Stoney, but this was a middle-aged man. He curtly introduced himself as Al. "What can I do for you?"

Sharon swallowed. "I'm Ione." Her voice came out a whisper.

"Huh?"

She drew in a breath. "I'm Ione," she said more clearly.

Al lifted his eyes toward the ceiling. "Yeah, sure. We're going to have to hire an extra receptionist just to take care of all the Ione's showing up. You won't catch the worm just because you're early, you know." He got out a pad of paper and a pen from the nearby desk.

"I really am Ione," she said. He handed her the pad and pen. "Prove it. Write 'You might lose your allergy to marriage' and sign it."

Her hand was quivering. She hoped it wouldn't alter her handwriting. She had trouble holding the pen. "Can I sit down? I feel a little shaky."

He motioned to the chair behind the desk. "You Stoney fans sure take things seriously."

Sharon ignored the comment. She sat down, closed her eyes for a moment and breathed deeply. Then she wrote the line he requested and signed it Ione. She tore the sheet off the pad and handed it to Al.

Al got a key from his pocket and opened a file drawer nearby. He took out a manila folder and when he opened it, she saw her letters inside. Al picked up the top one, Ione's short, final letter, and compared it to Sharon's handwriting, his expression impatient and remotely amused.

As his eyes moved from one paper to the other, he blinked. He set the sheets down on the desk and turned the small desk lamp on them. "Good grief!" He looked up at her. "You mean, you're real?"

She made a weak smile. "'Fraid so."

His expression had changed to one of excitement. "No, no, this is . . . wait here!" He grabbed the letter and the paper and ran down the hall, leaving her alone. The radio was piped into the room and a hit song was playing. She knew Stoney was somewhere close by. Sharon wrung her hands, wondering what would happen next.

In moments, Al came back with another man—again not Stoney, but a young fellow with a brown beard. Al introduced him as Harve. Harve had a stopwatch hanging from his neck. He looked at her with wide eyes, taking in every feature of her face.

"Glad to meet you, Ione. Stoney's waiting. I'll take you in."

"Where?"

"The studio, where Stoney's doing his show."

She shook her head in horror. "I'm not going in there. He'd probably put me on the air!"

"Of course! That's the point." He glanced at his stopwatch. "Come on. There's only twelve seconds till this song ends."

So Stoney *was* doing this for publicity. As Harve grabbed her by the hand, she decided she had little choice at this point but to fall into Stoney's trap. She steeled herself for humiliation, knowing Stoney would enjoy himself thoroughly at her expense and get huge ratings in the process. *Keep your head,* she told herself as Harve pulled her down the hall. Maybe there was some way she could get a few digs back at Stoney. Oh, God, she wished this was all over.

They came to the glass door of a glass enclosure. Sharon could see Stoney inside. He turned from the equipment in front of him when he glimpsed them through the glass. Tearing off his earphones, he set them around his neck as he watched them come in.

"Here she is!" Harve said, smiling triumphantly as he held up her hand in victory.

Stoney gave her a hard stare. "It's about time you showed up!" He motioned to her authoritatively. "Come here."

"What for?" she asked, balking at going any farther into the room.

"Come here!" Stoney unplugged the earphones, attached by wire to the equipment, and stepped up to her. She tried to back away into the glass, but he slipped his arm around her waist and made her walk with him to his swivel chair. He sat down and pulled her onto his lap.

Harve watched them in fascinated amazement.

"Time?" Stoney shouted, plugging in his earphones again.

Harve fumbled with his stopwatch. "One second." He rushed to the empty chair next to Stoney's.

Stoney pressed a button and adjusted the microphone in front of them, so that it was closer to Sharon. He slipped the earphones on his head again.

"Guess what?" he said to the microphone, sounding a little stunned. "She's here. Ione has finally shown up!"

Sharon gulped and leaned away from the mike, but Stoney held her in place on his lap.

"Her handwriting's been checked. Not that that was necessary. I knew all along, from the very beginning, who she was."

Sharon was incensed. "You did not!" she muttered.

"Say it into the microphone." His hand at her back pushed her closer to the metal bulb.

She made herself be brave, remembering her vow to get her own digs in. "You didn't know I was Ione at first. It was only since you found my written quiz from class, wasn't it?"

Stoney nodded. "I stand corrected. See, she and I are in a class together." He looked at Sharon. "Tell them who you are. Your real name."

She turned a bit to glare at him. He pointed at the microphone.

"Sharon Harper," she said.

"Yes, Sharon Harper of Wanna Be's. She's the lady who called me Numbnuts, remember?"

Sharon winced, preparing for his eager darts.

"Now," he went on, "how and why did you turn yourself into Ione?"

She hesitated. "Because..."

"Louder."

"To get back at you."

He seemed surprised. "Get back at me?"

"You made fun of me on your show because I'd called you Numb—...because I'd called you that. And you made fun of Wanna Be's, too. I felt I had no recourse, so I...I started writing those letters. I thought if Ione could give you your just comeuppance, I'd be satisfied."

"I see," Stoney said. "And were you?"

"Satisfied? No. You ignored the point I was trying to make and kept asking me to write again and again."

Stoney seemed amused. "So, why did you?"

Sharon had no good answer. "I don't know," she replied, sounding a bit like a child being asked to explain her actions to a parent.

He grinned. "How did you come up with the name, Ione?" he asked, his voice full of curiosity.

"It's my middle name. Sharon Ione Harper."

"Now, why didn't I think to ask you your middle name?" he said ruefully.

"I wouldn't have told you. I've always thought it was a silly name." It was odd, but she didn't have the sense that a huge audience was listening. She felt as if she were speaking only to Stoney. Maybe it was the way his eyes were focused on her, as if no one else in the world existed.

"I think it's a beautiful name," Stoney said.

Harve tapped him and pointed to his stopwatch. Stoney nodded at him.

"Before we go to commercial, I have one more question to ask you, Ione. Our listeners are waiting with bated breath for your answer." Stoney adjusted the microphone again, looking a little nervous. She could see his hand trembling a bit. He cleared his throat. "Will you marry me?"

Sharon couldn't believe this. Here she was, sitting on his lap, on the air, and she was supposed to answer such a question? She didn't even know if he was serious.

There was only one way to find out—call his bluff.

"Sure," she said blithely.

Now he was the one who seemed unable to decipher truth from fiction. "You mean that?"

"If you do," she replied, giving him a taste of his own evasive tactic.

"Well," he said uneasily, "I do mean it. Set a date."

She didn't know if his uneasiness stemmed from the fact that she'd called his bluff and he was getting himself in too deep with his hoax, or because he wasn't sure if *she* was sincere. "A date?" she said. "Okay. One month from today."

"That's not much time to find a church and a place for the reception..." he said, as if thinking aloud. "Of course, we could go to Tahoe or Las Vegas instead, couldn't we? All right, I'll go for that."

Sharon was beginning to feel a little dizzy. This whole thing was getting surreal. He sounded so genuine, she almost believed him.

Stoney studied her face, then said to the microphone, "She's looking a little pale. Our Ione's turning into a shrinking violet here." Then he said to her, "Is this a surprise? It shouldn't be. You wrote in your last letter that you'd make me lose my allergy to marriage.''

"I . . . I thought that would scare you off."

"No way."

"Why not? Why are you doing this?"

"What?"

"Proposing on the air?"

"I love you, Sharon. I want everybody to know."

Sharon could hardly believe he'd actually said the word *love*. To *her*. Emotion welled up inside and she bit her lip as she broke into tears.

Stoney held her as she wept into his shoulder, and he told his audience, "She's having a little cry. We'll cut to a commercial." Harve pressed a button, and a recording came on. Stoney hit the button to turn off the microphone and took off his headset.

"Are you okay?" Stoney asked her.

"Yes," she said, sitting straight again. Annoyed with herself, wondering if she was being gullible for believing him, she dried her tears with her hands. "I didn't sleep all night and I'm tired, that's all. If you really loved me, why didn't you tell me sooner? Why wait till now? For the publicity?"

"No! Because you hadn't been straight with me about Ione. After I found out, I waited, gave you opportunities to tell me the truth, but you didn't. I felt you must not trust me much if you didn't have the confidence to tell me. I didn't want to prod you this way, but our relationship was beginning to suffer, and I wanted the problem to end. So I tried to find a way to make you 'fess up. I was getting desperate, and I do have a tendency toward public spectacle when I'm on the air. I just wanted you to finally admit you were Ione, so we didn't have that big secret between us. You got nervous every time I mentioned her."

"You took a while before you told me you were Stoney, not Stanton," she declared in her defense.

"But I did confess of my own volition. Why didn't you?"

She looked down at her hands in her lap, feeling ashamed. Stoney took hold of one hand and squeezed it.

"I was too embarrassed," she said. "I wrote the first letter on a whim and in a temper. I didn't think you would carry it so far."

"It was a great letter," he said.

"Ohhh." She waved her free hand dismissively.

"Sharon, when I got home, looked at your quiz again and realized the handwriting was very familiar, I was astonished—not just at the fact that you and Ione were the same, but that you could verbally take me on the way you did."

"You seemed to win every round," she said.

"I didn't feel that way. It took all my ingenuity and creativity to answer you back." He chuckled. "But I should have known the lady with the sassy scissors shouldn't be underestimated."

Sharon smiled. She touched his thumb. "So what now?"

"We get married in a month."

She looked up. "You mean you're really . . . you're serious about that?"

"Yes!" He grasped her shoulders and gently shook her. "I just told a million people I'd marry you—what did you think?"

"I thought it was a publicity stunt."

"Sharon, even *I* wouldn't carry publicity that far."

"But you told me that if Stoney Ross got married it would be—"

"A major public event," he said, finishing the sentence for her. "I meant that when we got married, it would certainly make news, at QWIN anyway." He hesitated, and a shadow crossed his eyes. "You mean, you weren't serious about your answer because you thought it was a stunt? You were just playing along?"

"Well, yes, I was just playing along."

The glow in his eyes dimmed. His shoulders slackened. "Oh..."

She slipped her arms around his neck. "It's okay. I've been hoping you'd ask me to marry you. But you'd always made it clear you were a confirmed bachelor, so I was afraid to keep on hoping." She smiled as she saw shimmery lights coming into his eyes. "If you want to marry me, that's fine with me. That's perfect."

She kissed him then, softly and tenderly.

Harve cleared his throat. "Three seconds, Stoney."

Sharon broke the kiss and leaned out of the way while Stoney scrambled to get his headphones back on. Harve turned on the microphone and did the countdown for him, holding up three fingers, two, one, then none. Stoney stared blankly at the mike for a long second. Nothing was going out over the air. Harve gestured, waving his hand in circles as if trying to get Stoney going.

"I can't think of a thing to say," Stoney finally told his radio audience. "I just kissed the woman I love. She's going to marry me. My mind's blown!"

Harve cracked up laughing, and Sharon looked at Stoney with wide eyes.

"Maybe I should use this moment to wax philosophical—a new trend for me," Stoney continued, apparently pulling his thoughts together. "I always said I was allergic to marriage, and I believed that. I didn't know I wanted to get married until I met Sharon Ione Harper. But now that she and I are permanently together, we're going to be a terrific team. She's got Wanna Be's, the best styling salon in the state, and I've got the best morning radio show here at QWIN. Together we're unbeatable, so Southern California had better watch out! Now, how about a love song?" He pressed a button and a Michael Bolton ballad came on. Slowly he took off his earphones.

Touched by his words, Sharon was quiet for a moment. "I'd better go to work," she said softly.

He nodded in agreement. "You'd better, both for Wanna Be's sake and for mine. I can't think with you here. See you later? I'll stop by the salon when my show's over. Maybe we can have lunch together."

"Tuesday's a slower day. I can probably arrange it," she said. She kissed him warmly on the mouth and felt his response. "What about tonight?" she whispered, glancing at Harve, who was pretending to ignore them.

"Come over as soon as you're off. I'll be waiting."

Sharon got up from his lap, said goodbye to Harve, kissed Stoney again and left the station. As she walked to her car, she had that curious feeling of her feet not quite touching the pavement. She had everything she wanted now, a great love and a successful career. And it was Stoney who had made the difference in her life.

When she got into her car, she turned on the radio to hear his voice as she drove to work. She had the comfortable feeling of knowing that she'd hear that voice, on and off radio, for the rest of her life.

* * * * *

SILHOUETTE® *Desire*®

Do you want...

Dangerously handsome heroes

Evocative, everlasting love stories

Sizzling and tantalizing sensuality

Incredibly sexy miniseries like **MAN OF THE MONTH**

Red-hot romance

Enticing entertainment that can't be beat!

You'll find all of this, and much *more* each and every month in **SILHOUETTE DESIRE**. Don't miss these unforgettable love stories by some of romance's hottest authors. Silhouette Desire—where your fantasies will always come true....

DES-GEN

If you've got the time...
We've got the
INTIMATE MOMENTS

Passion. Suspense. Desire. Drama. Enter a world that's larger than life, where men and women overcome life's greatest odds for the ultimate prize: love. Nonstop excitement is closer than you think...in Silhouette Intimate Moments!

What's a single dad to do when he needs a wife by next Thursday?

Who's a confirmed bachelor to call when he finds a baby on his doorstep?

How does a plain Jane in love with her gorgeous boss get him to notice her?

From classic love stories to romantic comedies to emotional heart tuggers, **Silhouette Romance** offers six irresistible novels every month by some of your favorite authors!

Such as...beloved bestsellers **Diana Palmer, Annette Broadrick, Suzanne Carey, Elizabeth August** and **Marie Ferrarella**, to name just a few—and some sure to become favorites!

Fabulous Fathers...Bundles of Joy...Miniseries... Months of blushing brides and convenient weddings... Holiday celebrations... You'll find all this and much more in **Silhouette Romance**—always emotional, always enjoyable, always about love!

STEP

INTO

THE

A collection of award-winning books
by award-winning authors!
From Harlequin and Silhouette.

Available this April

TOGETHER ALWAYS

by DALLAS SCHULZE

Voted Best American Romance—
Reviewer's Choice Award

Award-winning author Dallas Schulze brings you the romantic
tale of two people destined to be together. From the moment
he laid eyes on her, Trace Dushane knew he had but one
mission in life...to protect beautiful Lily. He promised to save
her from disaster, but could he save her from himself?

Dallas Schulze is "one of today's most exciting authors!"
                                              —Barbara Bretton

Available this April wherever Harlequin books are sold.

SILHOUETTE... Where Passion Lives

Don't miss these Silhouette favorites by some of our most distinguished authors! And now you can receive a discount by ordering two or more titles!

SD#05849	MYSTERY LADY by Jackie Merritt	$2.99	☐
SD#05867	THE BABY DOCTOR	$2.99 U.S.	☐
	by Peggy Moreland	$3.50 CAN.	☐
IM#07610	SURROGATE DAD	$3.50 U.S.	☐
	by Marion Smith Collins	$3.99 CAN.	☐
IM#07616	EYEWITNESS	$3.50 U.S.	☐
	by Kathleen Creighton	$3.99 CAN.	☐
SE#09934	THE ADVENTURER	$3.50 U.S.	☐
	by Diana Whitney	$3.99 CAN.	☐
SE#09916	AN INTERRUPTED MARRIAGE	$3.50 U.S.	☐
	by Laurey Bright	$3.99 CAN.	☐
SR#19050	MISS SCROOGE	$2.75 U.S.	☐
	by Toni Collins	$3.25 CAN.	☐
SR#08994	CALEB'S SON	$2.75	☐
	by Laurie Paige		
YT#52001	WANTED: PERFECT PARTNER	$3.50 U.S.	☐
	by Debbie Macomber	$3.99 CAN.	☐
YT#52002	LISTEN UP, LOVER	$3.50 U.S.	☐
	by Lori Herter	$3.99 CAN.	☐

(limited quantities available on certain titles)

TOTAL AMOUNT	$ _____	
DEDUCT: 10% DISCOUNT FOR 2+ BOOKS	$ _____	
POSTAGE & HANDLING	$ _____	
($1.00 for one book, 50¢ for each additional)		
APPLICABLE TAXES**	$ _____	
TOTAL PAYABLE	$ _____	
(check or money order—please do not send cash)		

To order, send the completed form with your name, address, zip or postal code, along with a check or money order for the total above, payable to Silhouette Books, to: **In the U.S.:** 3010 Walden Avenue, P.O. Box 9077, Buffalo, NY 14269-9077; **In Canada:** P.O. Box 636, Fort Erie, Ontario, L2A 5X3.

Name:_____

Address:_____ City:_____

State/Prov.:_____ Zip/Postal Code:_____

**New York residents remit applicable sales taxes.
Canadian residents remit applicable GST and provincial taxes.   SBACK-MM2

ᔐ Silhouette®

"Motherhood is full of love, laughter
and sweet surprises. Silhouette's collection
is every bit as much fun!"
—Bestselling author Ann Major

This May, treat yourself to...

WANTED:

MOTHER

Silhouette's annual tribute to motherhood takes a
new twist in '96 as three sexy single men prepare for
fatherhood—and saying "I Do!" This collection makes
the perfect gift, not just for moms but for all romance
fiction lovers! Written by these captivating authors:

Annette Broadrick
Ginna Gray
Raye Morgan

"The Mother's Day anthology from Silhouette is the
highlight of any romance lover's spring!"
—Award-winning author **Dallas Schulze**

MD96